Allegra was too stunned to say a word.

At twenty-one Xavier Lefèvre had been a good-looking boy. At thirty-one he was all man. A little taller, unless her memory deceived her, and his frame was broader—though his T-shirt showed that it was muscle rather than fat. His olive skin made his gray-green eyes seem even more piercing, and he had the beginnings of lines around his eyes, as if he smiled a lot or spent most of his time in the sun. His tousled dark hair was overlong; the style, she thought, was more in keeping with a rock star than a financial whiz kid. And the fact that he hadn't shaved made him look as if he'd just got out of bed, leaving his lover asleep and totally satiated.

Just the sight of him made Allegra feel as if the temperature in the room had soared by ten degrees—she could still remember just how it had felt to fall asleep in Xav's arms, warm and satiated in the sunshine, after making love all afternoon.

How was she supposed to think straight, when the first thing that came into her mind where Xavier Lefèvre was concerned was sex—and the second thing was how much she still wanted him?

She needed her libido strapped into a straitjacket. Right now. Before it started wrestling with her common sense.

KATE HARDY lives in Norwich, in the east of England, with her husband, two young children and too many books to count! When she's not busy writing romance or researching local history, she helps out at her children's schools; she's a school governor and chair of the PTA. She also loves cooking—see if you can spot the recipes sneaked into her books! (They're also on her website, along with extracts and stories behind the books.)

Writing for Harlequin Books has been a dream come true for Kate—something she's wanted to do ever since she was twelve. She's been writing Harlequin® Medical Romance novels for more than seven years now, and also writes for Harlequin Presents. She says it's the best of both worlds, because she gets to learn lots of new things when she's researching the background to a book—add a touch of passion, drama and danger, a new gorgeous hero every time, and it's the perfect job!

Kate's always delighted to hear from readers, so do drop in to her website at www.katehardy.com.

Xavier Lefèvre (the hero of this novel) has an equally attractive brother. Meet him in Kate Hardy's next book for Harlequin Presents Extra— on sale in January 2011!

RED WINE AND HER SEXY EX

KATE HARDY

~ Unfinished Business ~

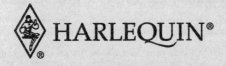

HARLEQUIN®

TORONTO • NEW YORK • LONDON
AMSTERDAM • PARIS • SYDNEY • HAMBURG
STOCKHOLM • ATHENS • TOKYO • MILAN • MADRID
PRAGUE • WARSAW • BUDAPEST • AUCKLAND

Recycling programs
for this product may
not exist in your area.

ISBN-13: 978-0-373-52795-3

RED WINE AND HER SEXY EX

First North American Publication 2010.

RED WINE AND
HER SEXY EX

For Maggie—who helped me see the wood for the trees—with love and thanks.

CHAPTER ONE

SHE was back.

Xavier's heart beat just that little bit faster as he put down the phone to his lawyer.

This was ridiculous. He was completely over Allegra Beauchamp. He'd been over her for years. So of course it wasn't nerves making his pulse race like this. It was anger—anger that she was planning to walk in after all this time and interfere. He'd put his heart and soul into the vineyard for the last ten years, and he was damn sure he wasn't going to let her flounce in and ruin all his hard work.

He didn't trust her a single millimetre. Not any more. Quite apart from the way she'd broken his heart, dumping him when he'd needed her most, she hadn't come back to support her great-uncle—the man who'd given her a home every summer while she was growing up—when he'd been old and frail and needed her. She hadn't even made it back to France for Harry's funeral; but she'd come straight back to claim her inheritance of fifteen hectares of top-quality vines and a big stone *mas*.

Her actions spoke volumes.

But in some ways it also made things easier. If Allegra was only interested in the money, then she'd be happy to sell her half of the vineyard to him, despite what she'd claimed to his lawyer this afternoon. Right now, she might have some romantic idea of what it was like to run a vineyard, but Xavier knew that as soon as she had a taste of the real thing she'd run straight back to London. Just as she had ten years ago—except this time she'd only be taking his money with her, not his heart. And this time he'd have no regrets.

He grabbed his car keys from his desk drawer, locked his office door and strode off towards his car. The sooner he faced her, the better.

Allegra sipped her coffee, but the dark, bitter liquid did nothing to clear her head.

She'd been a fool to come back after all this time. She should've just agreed with the lawyer's suggestion of selling Harry's half of the vineyard to his business partner, stopped off briefly at the tiny church in the village to lay some flowers on her great-uncle's grave and pay her respects, and then gone straight back to London.

Instead, something had made her come back to the old stone farmhouse where she'd spent so many summers as a child. Whether it was an impulse to do right by her great-uncle or something else, she wasn't sure. But now she was here in the Ardèche, she regretted the impulse. Seeing the house, smelling the sharp scent of the herbs growing in their terracotta troughs by the kitchen door, had made her feel physically sick with guilt. Guilt that she hadn't come back before. Guilt that she hadn't been there to take the call telling her that Harry had had a stroke—and that he'd died in hospital before she'd even found out that he was ill. Guilt that, despite her best efforts, she hadn't made it here for the funeral.

Everyone in the village had already judged her and found her wanting. She'd been aware of the glances and mutters from people in the square as she'd put the flowers on the greening-over mound in the churchyard, next to the little wooden cross that would mark Harry's grave until the ground had settled enough for it to support a proper headstone. And the coldness with which Hortense Bouvier had received her, instead of the warm hug and good meal that the housekeeper had greeted her with all those years before, had left her in no doubt as to the older woman's disapproval.

Walking back into the kitchen had been like walking straight back into the past, ripping all of Allegra's scars wide open. All she needed now was Xav to walk into the kitchen and drop into the chair opposite her, with that heart-turning smile and the sparkle in his silver-green eyes as he reached over to take her hand, and…

No, of course not. He'd made it quite clear, ten years before, that it was over between them. That what they'd shared had simply been a holiday romance, and he was off to start a high-flying career in Paris—a new life without her. For all she knew, he could be married with children now; once she'd taken that first step to heal the breach between herself and Harry, they'd had an unspoken agreement never to talk about Xavier. Pride had stopped her asking, and awkwardness had stopped Harry telling.

Her hands tightened round the mug of coffee. After all these years, she really should be over it. But then again, how did you stop years and years of loving someone? She'd fallen for Xavier Lefèvre the very first time she'd met him, when she was eight years old and he was eleven: he'd been the most beautiful boy she'd ever seen, like one of the Victorian angels in the stained-glass windows at school, but with dark hair and silver-green eyes. As a teen, she'd followed him round like an eager puppy, mooning over him and wondering what it would be like if he kissed her. She'd even practised kissing against the back of her hand so she'd be ready for the moment when he finally realised she was more than just the girl next door. For summer after summer, she'd wished and hoped; even though she must have driven him crazy, he'd been kind and treated her the same way that he treated everyone else, never teasing or rejecting her outright.

But, that very last summer, it had been a kind of awakening. Xav had finally seen her as a woman instead of an annoying little urchin trailing around behind him. They'd been inseparable. The best summer of her life. She'd honestly believed that he loved her as much as she loved him. That it didn't matter that she was going to do her degree in London while he was starting a new job in Paris—she'd spend the holidays with him, and he'd maybe come and spend weekends with her in London when he could get the time off work, and then when she graduated they'd be together for the rest of their lives.

Granted, he hadn't actually asked her to marry him, but she'd known he felt the same way she did. That he was as crazy about her as she was about him.

And then it had all disintegrated.

Bile filled her mouth and she swallowed hard. For pity's sake. She was an adult, now, not a dream-filled teenager. A realist. Harry's business partner was Jean-Paul Lefèvre—Xav's father, not Xav himself. Xav wouldn't be here; as far as she knew, he was still in Paris. She wouldn't have to see him again.

'Monsieur Lefèvre called,' Hortense said coolly, walking into the kitchen. 'He's on his way back from the vines. He's calling in to see you.'

Allegra frowned. Their meeting wasn't until tomorrow. Then again, the French had impeccable manners. Jean-Paul was probably calling on her out of politeness, to welcome her to Les Trois Closes.

And then the kitchen door opened abruptly and Xavier sauntered in, as if he owned the place.

Allegra nearly dropped the mug she was holding. What the hell was *he* doing here? And why hadn't he knocked? What made him think that he could just walk into Harry's house—*her* house, she corrected herself mentally—whenever he pleased?

'Xavier! *Alors*, sit down, sit down.' Hortense greeted him with all the warmth she'd refused to bestow on Allegra, kissing him on the cheeks. She settled him opposite Allegra with a mug of coffee. 'I'll leave you to talk with Mademoiselle Beauchamp, *chéri*.' And with that she swept out of the kitchen.

Allegra was too stunned to say a word. At twenty-one, Xavier Lefèvre had been a good-looking boy. At thirty-one, he was all man. A little taller, unless her memory deceived her, and his frame was broader—though his T-shirt showed that it was muscle rather than fat. His olive skin made his grey-green eyes seem even more piercing, and he had the beginnings of lines round his eyes, as if he smiled a lot or spent most of his time in the sun. His tousled dark hair was overlong; the style, she thought, was more in keeping with a rock star than a financial whiz-kid. And the fact that he hadn't shaved made him look as if he'd just got out of bed, leaving his lover asleep and totally satiated.

Just the sight of him made Allegra feel as if the temperature in the room had soared by ten degrees—and she could still remember just how it had felt to fall asleep in Xav's arms, warm and satiated in the sunshine after making love all afternoon.

Oh, hell. How was she supposed to think straight when the first thing that came into her mind where Xavier Lefèvre was concerned was sex—and the second thing was how much she still wanted him?

She needed her libido strapped into a straightjacket. Right now. Before it started wrestling with her common sense.

'*Bonjour*, Mademoiselle Beauchamp.' Xavier gave her an enigmatic smile. 'I thought I'd better come and say hello to my new business partner.'

She stared at him, shocked. '*You* were Harry's business partner?'

His look told her just how stupid that question was.

'But…' Xavier was supposed to be a financier in a sharp suit, not a vigneron in faded denims and an ancient T-shirt. 'I thought you were in Paris.'

'No.'

'Monsieur Robert said Harry's partner was Monsieur Lefèvre.'

'Indeed.' Still seated, he pantomimed a half-bow. 'Allow me to introduce myself. Xavier Lefèvre—at your service, *mademoiselle*.'

'I know who you are.' For pity's sake. Of *course* she knew who he was. The man to whom she'd given her virginity—and her heart, only to have it thrown back in her face. 'I thought he meant your father.'

'You're five years too late for that, I'm afraid.'

'Your father's...?' She sucked in a shocked breath. 'I'm sorry. I had no idea. Harry didn't tell me, or I would've—'

'Don't tell me you would've come to my father's funeral,' Xavier cut in. 'You didn't even turn up to Harry's.'

And he thought he had the right to call her on it? She lifted her chin. 'I had my reasons.'

He said nothing. Waiting for her to fill the silence? Well, she didn't have to explain herself to him. 'So, what—you thought that as you're his business partner Harry should have left the vineyard to you? Is that it?'

'No, of course not. There's no question of that. You inherit his possessions because you're his closest family.' He paused. 'Not that anyone would have guessed, these last few years.'

'That's a cheap shot.' And it had landed dead on target. Smack in the middle of her guilt, like a hard blow on an already spreading bruise.

'Just stating the facts, *chérie*. When was the last time you came back to see him?'

'I spoke to him every week on the phone.'

'Which isn't the same thing at all.'

She blew out a breath. 'You probably know Harry and I fell out pretty badly after I went to London.' Over Xavier—not that she was going to tell him that. 'We made it up eventually, but I admit I was wrong not to come back and see him.' Especially as half the reason had been the fear that she might have to see Xavier again. Not that she had any intention of admitting that to him, either. She didn't want him to have a clue that she still had a weak spot where he was concerned. That seeing him again had knocked her for six and the old, old longing hadn't died at all—it had just been sleeping, and now it was awake again and desperately hungry for him. 'If I'd had any idea that he was so frail, I would've come back. He didn't give me the faintest clue.'

'Of course not. He was a proud man. But if you'd bothered visiting,' Xavier said coolly, 'you would've seen it for yourself.'

There was no answer to that.

'You didn't come back when he was ill,' Xavier continued.

'Because I didn't get the message that he'd had a stroke until after it was too late.'

'You didn't even turn up for his funeral.'

And he seriously thought she wasn't bothered about that? 'I intended to be here. But I was on business in New York.'

'Not good enough.'

She knew that. And she didn't need him to tell her. She lifted her chin. 'We've established that I'm firmly in the wrong. And it's not possible to change the past, so there's no point in rehashing it.'

He simply shrugged.

Infuriating man.

'What do you want, Xavier?'

You.

The realisation shocked him to the core. After the way Allegra had let him down, he shouldn't want anything to do with her. And she was no longer the *petite rose Anglaise* she'd been at eighteen, sweet and shy and a little unsure of herself and then blossoming under his love. Right now she was impeccably groomed and as hard as diamonds beneath that smart business suit. Her mouth was in a tight line, not soft and promising and reminding him of the first roses of summer.

This was crazy. For pity's sake, he was supposed to be working out how to get the woman to sell her half of the business to him, not looking at her mouth and remembering how it had felt to kiss her. How it had felt to lose himself inside her. How it had felt to see her expression soften and her eyes sparkle with love when she looked up from the book she was reading and caught him watching her, on those drowsy summer afternoons.

Oh, *Dieu*. He really had to get a grip.

'Well?'

'I just happened to be on my way back from the fields. I called Hortense to see if you were in, because I was going to be neighbourly and polite and welcome you back to France.' That was true—though it wasn't the whole truth. He'd also wanted to see if he could gauge her reactions. To work out a plan for persuading her to sell the vineyard to him. 'But, seeing as you raised the subject, let me give you something to think about. You haven't been to France in years and I can't see you being interested in the vineyard now. I'm more than happy to buy you out. Consult whatever qualified oenologist you like to get a price and I'll abide by his or her decision— I'll even pay the survey fee.'

'No.'

She wanted more than a fair price? Well, if it would keep his vineyard safe, it was worth paying over the odds. 'How much do you want?'

'I'm not selling the vineyard to you.'

His stomach turned. 'You're planning to sell to someone else?' To someone who would neglect the vines, so they'd end up diseased and it would spread into his fields? Or, worse, to someone who decided to use pesticide sprays and to hell with the neighbours—when it had taken him years to get organic certification for the vineyard. All that work could be ruined in a matter of weeks.

'I'm not selling to anyone. Harry left me the house and his half of the vineyard. The way I see it, this was his way of telling me it was time to come home,' Allegra said.

He waved a dismissive hand. 'That's guilt talking.' Guilt that he'd just encouraged, admittedly. 'You know as well as I do, the practical thing to do here would be to sell your share to me.'

She shook her head. 'I'm staying.'

He stared at her, incredulous. 'But you know nothing about viticulture.'

'I can learn.'

'I don't have time to teach you.'

'Then maybe someone else can.'

Over his dead body.

'And in the meantime I can deal with the marketing—it's what I'm trained to do.'

Xavier folded his arms, goaded into reacting. 'I don't care what you're trained to do. You're not dabbling in my vineyard. You'll get bored within a week.'

'No, I won't. And it's my vineyard, too.' She folded her arms, reflecting his own defensive body language, and glared at him. 'Harry left his half of the business to me, and I owe it to him to make it work.' Her blue eyes were distinctly icy, and Xavier realised that she was serious. She really did want to make this work, for Harry's sake.

Impossible; but, right now, she looked too stubborn and defensive to listen to common sense. So it would be better to leave now, think about the best tactics to make her see reason and talk to her again tomorrow.

'As you wish,' he said. He pushed his chair back and stood up. 'Did Marc tell you the time of the meeting tomorrow?'

She blinked. 'You're on first-name terms with Harry's lawyer?'

'Actually, he's my lawyer, too.' Xavier judged it politic not to mention that Marc had been his best friend since university. Though he did owe it to Marc to be fair. 'Although, I should add that he isn't acting for me in this case and he hasn't discussed you with me. Marc's the most professional man I know.'

'He said eight o'clock tomorrow morning.'

'Better make it midday,' Xavier said. 'I'm sure you're tired after all your travelling.'

Her eyes narrowed with suspicion. 'You don't think I'm capable of getting up early, do you?'

'I didn't say that.' Though he'd thought it. 'Actually, it would suit me better, too. Here, we work to *l'heure solaire.*'

'The time of the sun?' Her translation was hesitant.

'Sun time,' he corrected. 'Working on the vines in the middle of a summer day is the quickest way to get sunstroke. I do my admin in the hottest hours of the day and I work outside when it's a little cooler. So—midday. My office, at the chateau. And I will provide lunch.' He thought about kissing her goodbye on the cheek, just to unsettle her a little more—but then thought better of it. Given his body's earlier reaction to her, there was just as good a chance that it'd unsettle him, too. Instead, he gave her a formal bow. '*À demain*, Mademoiselle Beauchamp.'

She nodded in acknowledgement. '*À demain*, Monsieur Lefèvre. Midday it is.'

CHAPTER TWO

THE next morning, Allegra spent a while looking at the vineyard's website and jotting down some ideas before setting out for the Lefèvre chateau. The building had barely changed in the years she'd been away; it was still grand and imposing, pale stone punctuated by tall, narrow windows with white shutters. She remembered the formal lawn in front of the chateau, though she didn't remember there being lavender fields flanking the long driveway. And she was also fairly sure there hadn't been a rose garden at the back—although she couldn't see it when she got out of the car, the scent of roses was strong enough for her to guess that there was a mass of blooms somewhere behind the house.

Xavier's wife's idea, maybe?

Not that it was any of her concern. And she couldn't exactly have asked Hortense without it seeming like fishing—which it wasn't. Yes, Xavier Lefèvre was still the most attractive man Allegra had ever met. If it was possible, he'd got even better-looking with age. But, even if he wasn't involved with anyone, she wasn't interested. Wasn't going to give him a second chance to stamp on her heart. This was strictly business.

She glanced at her watch. Two minutes to midday. Not so early that she'd seem desperate, but early enough to tell Xavier that she was professional and punctual. Good. She straightened her back and rang the doorbell.

She had to ring twice more before the door was opened abruptly by a young man with a shock of fair hair who looked annoyed that he'd been disturbed.

'We're not—' he began with a scowl, then stopped and gave her a beaming smile. '*Mon Dieu, c'est* Allie Beauchamp! How long has it been? *Bonjour, chérie.* How are you?' He leaned forward to kiss her cheek.

'*Bonjour*, Guy. About ten years—and I'm fine, thanks.' She smiled back. 'It's good to see you. How are you?'

'Fine. It's good to see you, too. Are you here on holiday?' he asked.

'Not exactly.' She grimaced. 'I'm your brother's new business partner.'

Guy raised an eyebrow. 'Hmm.'

'Care to elaborate on that?' she asked.

'No. You know Xav.'

That was the point. She didn't, any more.

'At this time of day, he'll be in his office,' Guy said.

'I know.' Allegra shifted her weight to her other foot. 'I, um, forgot to ask him whereabouts in the estate his office was.'

'And he forgot to tell you.' Guy rolled his eyes. 'Typical Xav. I'll take you over there.'

'Are you going to be at the meeting?'

'Is it about the vineyard?'

She nodded.

'Then, no. The vineyard's Xav's department, not mine. I just laze about here at weekends, drink his wine and insult him.' He gave her an unrepentant grin. 'By the way, I'm sorry about Harry. He was a good man.'

Allegra had a huge lump in her throat. Guy was the first person in France who'd actually welcomed her warmly and used her old pet name. Maybe he remembered their childhood, when she'd persuaded Xav to include his little brother in their games. And he was the only one who hadn't treated her as a pariah for missing Harry's funeral. 'I'm sorry, too.'

Guy led her round the side of the house to a courtyard, which she remembered had once been stables and a barn but had now been turned into an office block.

'Thanks for bringing me over,' Allegra said.

'Pleasure.' He smiled at her. 'If you're going to be around for a few days, come and have dinner with us.'

'Us' meaning him and Xavier? She knew he was only being polite. Xavier definitely wouldn't second that invitation. 'That would be lovely,' she said, being equally polite.

'See you later, then. *À bientôt*, Allie.'

She echoed his farewell, took a deep breath, and walked into the office block. Xavier's door was wide open and she could see him working at his desk, making notes on something with a fountain pen. He looked deep in thought, with his left elbow resting on his desk and his forehead propped against his hand. His hair was tousled—obviously he'd been shoving his fingers through it—but today he was clean-shaven. The sleeves of his knitted cotton shirt were pushed up to his elbows, revealing strong forearms sprinkled with dark hair. Right at that moment, he looked approachable. Touchable. She had to dig her nails into her palms to stop herself doing something rash—like walking over to him, sliding her hand up his arm to get his attention, cupping his chin, and lowering her mouth to his, the way she once would have done.

For pity's sake. He wasn't her lover any more, the man she'd thought she'd marry one day. He was her business partner. And, even if he hadn't been her business partner, she had no idea whether or not he was already committed elsewhere. That made him absolutely off limits.

She took a deep breath, then knocked on the door.

Xavier looked up at Allegra's knock. She was clearly still in businesswoman mode, wearing another of those sharp suits. No way would she fit in here; at this time of year, everyone had to help out in the vines, maintaining the shoots and weeding under the vines. Next month would be pruning and then letting the grapes ripen, ready for harvest in late September. Among the vines, her business suit would be ripped to shreds, and those patent high-heeled shoes were completely unsuitable for the fields.

She really had no idea, did she?

'Thank you for coming,' he said, rising politely from his desk. 'Take a seat.'

She sat down, then handed him a gold box tied with a gold chiffon ribbon. 'For you.'

Now that he hadn't expected.

'I thought this might be more suitable than flowers. Or, um, wine.'

So she remembered French customs, then, of bringing a gift for your host. '*Merci*, Allegra.' He untied the ribbon and discovered that the box held his favourite weakness: thin discs of dark chocolate studded with crystallised ginger. She remembered such a tiny thing, after all these years? And she must've bought it this morning: he recognised the box as coming from Nicole's shop in the village. She'd made a real effort, and it knocked him completely off balance.

'Thank you,' he said again. 'Would you like some coffee?'

'Yes, please.'

To his surprise, she followed him into the tiny kitchen area. 'Anything I can do?'

Yes. Sell me your half of the vineyard and get out of my life before I go crazy with wanting you again. He just about stopped himself saying it. 'No need.'

'Aren't you going to ask me if I take milk and sugar?'

'You never used to, and it's obvious you still don't.'

She blinked. 'Obvious, how?'

He spread his hands. 'You wouldn't be so thin if you did.'

Her eyes narrowed. 'That's a bit personal.'

'You asked,' he pointed out.

'Gloves off, now?'

'They were never on in the first place.' And now his mind was running on a really dangerous track. Gloves off. Clothes off. Allegra's shy, trusting smile as he'd undressed her for the very first time and she'd given herself to him completely.

Oh, *Dieu*. He really had to stop thinking about the past and concentrate on the present.

He finished making the coffee and placed it on a tray. He fished a bowl of tomatoes and a hunk of cheese from the fridge, then took a rustic loaf from a cupboard and placed them next to the coffee, along with two knives and two plates, before carrying the lot back to his office.

'Help yourself,' he said, gesturing to the food.

'Thank you.'

When she didn't make a move, he raised an eyebrow, broke a hunk off the bread, and cut himself a large slice of cheese. 'Forgive me for being greedy. I'm starving—I was working in the vines at six.'

'L'heure solaire.'

He smiled, oddly pleased that she'd remembered. He could still hear England in her accent, but at least she was trying. No doubt she hadn't spoken French in a long, long while.

'So what's the agenda?' she asked.

'We'll start with the sensible one—when are you going to sell me your half of the vineyard?'

'That's not on the agenda at all,' she said. 'Xav, why won't you give me a chance?'

How on earth could she not know that? Did he have to spell out to her that, the last time he'd needed her, she hadn't been there and he didn't want to put himself in that position again? He certainly didn't trust his own judgement where she was concerned. He'd spent a sleepless night brooding over the fact that he still wanted her just as much as he had when he was twenty-one; it was a weakness he really didn't need. 'Because you're not cut out to work here,' he prevaricated. 'Look at you. Designer clothes, flash car...'

'A perfectly normal business suit,' she corrected, 'and the car's not mine, it's a rental. You're judging me, Xav, and you're being unfair.'

Unfair? *He* hadn't been the one to walk away. The sheer injustice stung, and he had to make a real effort to hold back the surge of irritation. An effort that wasn't entirely successful. 'What do you expect, Allegra?'

'Everybody makes mistakes.'

Yes. And he had no intention of repeating his.

Clearly his thoughts showed in his expression, because she sighed. 'You're not even going to listen to me, are you?'

'You said it all yesterday.' And ten years ago. When she hadn't given him time to deal with the way his life had just imploded, and she'd dumped him.

'This isn't just a whim, you know.'

And then he noticed the shadows underneath her eyes. It looked as though he wasn't the only one who'd spent a sleepless night. No doubt she'd been reliving the memories, too, the bad ones that had all but wiped out the good. And he had to admit that it had taken courage for her to come back, knowing full well that everyone here would have judged her actions and found her very much wanting.

'All right,' he said grudgingly. 'Explain, and I'll listen.'

'Without interruptions?'

'I can't promise that. But I'll listen.'

'OK.' She took a sip of her coffee, as if she needed something to bolster her—though her plate was still empty, he noticed. 'Harry and I fell out pretty badly when I first left for London, and I swore I'd never come back to France again. By the time I graduated, I'd mellowed a bit, and I saw things a bit differently. I made it up with him. But I was settled in England, then. And I...' She bit her lip. 'Oh, forget it. There's no point in explaining. You wouldn't understand in a million years.'

'Now who's judging?'

She gave him a wry smile. 'OK. You asked for it. You grew up here, where your family has lived for...what, a couple of hundred years?'

'Something like that.'

'You always knew where you were when you woke up. You were secure. You knew you *belonged*.'

'Well, yes.' Even when he'd planned to go to Paris, he'd always known that he'd come back to the Ardèche and take over the vineyard. But he'd thought he'd have time to broaden his experience in business, first, see a bit of the world.

'It wasn't like that for me. When I was a child, I was dragged all over the world in my parents' wake—the orchestra would be on tour, or my mother would do a series of solo concerts and my father would be her accompanist. We never settled anywhere. The nannies never lasted long—they'd thought they'd have an opportunity to travel and see the world, but they didn't bargain on the fact that my parents worked all the time and expected them to do likewise. When they weren't on stage, they were practising and didn't want to be disturbed. My mother would sometimes practise until her fingers bled. And then, just as somewhere started to become home, we'd move on again.'

He could see old hurts blooming in Allegra's expression, and her struggle to keep them back. And suddenly he realised what she was trying to tell him. 'So once you'd settled in London, you had your own place. Roots.'

'Exactly. And I could run my life the way *I* wanted it to be. I wasn't being pushed around and told what to do by someone else all the time, however well meaning they were.' She looked relieved. 'Thank you for understanding.'

He blew out a breath. 'No, you were right in the first place. I still don't understand. Surely your family always come first?' It was what he'd always believed.

The way his family—with the notable exception of his mother—had always done things. If there was a problem, you worked together to fix it.

'I didn't say it was logical.' She looked away. 'There were other reasons why I didn't want to come back to France.'

'Me?' He really hadn't meant to say it, but the word just slipped out.

'You,' she confirmed.

Well, at least it was out in the open now. They could stop pussyfooting round the issue.

She clearly thought the same, because she said, 'I was hoping you wouldn't be here.'

He rolled his eyes. 'I've been Harry's business partner since Papa died. Surely you knew that?'

A muscle flickered in her jaw. 'We never discussed you.'

Was she saying that her falling-out with Harry had been over him? But he couldn't see why. It was pretty clear-cut: she'd been the one to call a halt to their affair, not him. And Xavier couldn't imagine Harry breaking Jean-Paul's confidence and telling Allegra what had been going on here—about the problems with the business and Chantal's desertion. Had Harry perhaps counselled her to give Xavier some space and time, and she'd reacted badly because she felt he was trying to push her around, the way she'd been pushed around as a child?

But he needed to know the answer to the most pressing question first. 'Why are you here now, Allegra?'

'Because I owe it to Harry. And don't waste your energy giving me a hard time over missing his funeral. It wasn't intentional and I feel guilty enough about it.'

'I don't have the right to judge you for that,' Xavier said quietly, 'but Harry was my friend as well as my business partner, and I think he deserved better.'

'I know he did.' Colour stained her cheeks.

'Surely your business wasn't *that* urgent? Why didn't you tell your boss or your business contact that you had a family commitment?'

'I did. The client couldn't move the meeting.'

'Couldn't someone else have gone in your place?'

'According to my boss, no.' Her tone was dry, and Xavier had a feeling that there was more to this—something she wasn't telling him. 'I did my best to wrap everything up as quickly as I could, but the meeting overran and I missed my flight.'

'And that was the only flight to Avignon?' he asked. As excuses went, that was a little too pat for his liking. Too convenient.

'Nice, actually,' she corrected. 'It was the only flight to France from New York without a stopover, until the next day. The reservations clerk spent an hour on the computer, trying to find me a flight that would get me somewhere on French soil at some time before breakfast, French time.' She spread her hands. 'But there simply wasn't one. Not even to Paris.'

'Your parents didn't turn up, either.'

'I know. They were in Tokyo. Coming to the funeral would've meant missing a performance. You know what they're like.' She lifted her chin. 'And, yes, you could say I fell into the same trap. I put business before family, and I shouldn't have done.'

'At least you admit it was a mistake.' He paused. 'So, where do you suggest we go from here?'

'You trusted Harry's business judgement, yes?'

Xavier inclined his head.

'And Harry trusted me to take over from him, or he wouldn't have left me his part of the business.' She looked him straight in the eye. 'So are you going to do the same?'

Tricky. He didn't trust his judgement at all, where she was concerned. And trusting her was one hell of an ask. He took refuge in answering a question with a question. 'What do you know about making wine?'

'Right now? Very little,' she admitted. 'But I'm a fast learner. I'll put in the hours until I know enough to be useful. In the meantime, maybe I can be useful in another part of the business.'

'Such as?'

'As I told you yesterday—marketing. I was Acting Head of Creative at the agency where I worked. I can put an effective promotional campaign together on a shoestring budget. Though I'll need some information from you before I can analyse how things are done now and where I can make a difference.'

'What kind of information?' he asked warily.

'The business plan for the next five years. I need to know what we produce, how much we sell it for, who our main customers are and how we get the wine to them.' She ticked them off on her fingers. 'I also need to know who our main competitors are and what they produce. And what kind of marketing campaigns you've done in the past. I know the vineyard has a website, but I want to look at that and compare it with the kind of thing our main competitors produce. And then I'll give you my analysis and recommendations.'

'Strengths, weaknesses, opportunities, threats.' He raised an eyebrow at her obvious surprise. 'Do you think I don't know what they are already?'

She looked deflated. And suddenly Xavier could see the vulnerability in her. On the surface, she was bright and polished and professional. But underneath she was as fragile as hell.

He could break her right now and make her sell her half of the vineyard to him.

But he'd hate himself for doing it. And, weirdly, he suddenly found himself wanting to protect her. How ironic was that? She'd broken his heart, and he still wanted to protect her; even though he couldn't protect himself from her. 'So are you telling me you're planning to run half a vineyard from London?'

'No. From here.'

She was planning to live here? So he'd have to see her every single day? *Dieu*—that would take some coping with. While she'd been in another country, he'd been able to push any thoughts of her to the back of his mind. But living next door to her, working with her...that would be a completely different matter.

And something didn't quite add up. 'Two minutes ago you were telling me that your roots were in London.'

'They are.' She sighed. 'I didn't say this was rational, Xav. It's just how it is. I want to step into Harry's shoes. As you just suggested, I can't do that from London. And the Ardèche was home to me in the summer, many years ago. I can settle here.'

Ten years too late. He'd wanted her here, by his side, back then. As his wife. Now, he'd be a lot happier if she flounced back to London and left him alone.

'What about your job?'

'Ex,' she said succinctly.

'Since when?'

'I resigned yesterday. After my meeting with my lawyer.'

So she was using the vineyard as some kind of get-out? In some respects, Xavier knew he could relax because it meant she wasn't planning to sell the land to someone else; but, in other respects, her statement made him even more tense. Was that how she reacted to pressure—by walking out and launching herself into something else? So what would happen if the going got tough here? Would she bail out, the way his mother had bailed out on his father? 'What about your notice period?'

'In my profession, you can do too much damage if you stay. If you decide to leave, you leave there and then.' She shrugged. 'My assistant's clearing my desk for me and I'll pick up my personal effects later.'

'Bit of a spur-of-the-moment decision, isn't it? How do you know this is going to work out?'

'Because I'm going to make it work out.'

Stubborn and determined: both were points in her favour. In this job, she'd need them. But he still couldn't believe that she'd stick to this. 'Running a vineyard isn't a nine-to-five job,' he warned. 'There are times when we all need to muck in and work on the vines—and what you're wearing right now is completely impractical for working in the fields. Your clothes will be shredded and your shoes—well, you'll turn your ankle or get blisters. And then there's the risk of sunstroke.'

'I'm not afraid of hard work or putting in the hours. Show me what needs to be done, and I'll do it. And I've already told you, I can do jeans and boots and a sunhat, if I have to.'

And doubtless hers would all be designer.

'I don't have Harry's knowledge or experience, so of course I'm not going to be able to fill his shoes,' she said. 'But I learn fast, and if I don't know something I'll ask—I won't just muddle through and hope for the best.'

'Perhaps I should also tell you that Harry was a sleeping partner in the business,' Xavier mused.

Her face shuttered. 'So you're *not* going to give me a chance.'

'That isn't what I said. Allegra, he was almost eighty. I was hardly going to make him work the same hours that I do. And he was happy to let me run the vineyard my way.'

'So what are you saying? That I can stay, but I get no input in anything?' She shook her head. 'No deal.'

'I wasn't offering you a deal. I'm telling you the way it is. Sure, I asked Harry for advice on some things—but I can't do that with you because, as you just said yourself, you don't have his knowledge or his experience.'

'And I also told you that I have other skills. Useful skills. If you give me the information I asked for, I'll work up some proposals. I can bring other things to the vineyard. Added value.'

Xavier took a deep breath. 'The information you're asking for is commercially sensitive.'

'And, as your business partner, I have no intention of letting that information out of my sight—because if it affects the business, it affects *me*.'

She really wasn't going to give up. He stared at her for a moment, weighing her up: could he trust her, this time round?

Harry had obviously trusted her, or he would've left instructions to handle his estate differently.

This was a huge, huge risk. But Harry had never steered him wrong before; and Marc had argued in her favour, too, in their phone call the previous day. And

Guy had actually left his precious lab for a few minutes to bring her over to the office. Harry, Marc and Guy were the three people Xavier trusted most, and they didn't seem to share his wariness of Allegra. So perhaps his best friend and his brother could see things more clearly, their judgement of her not clouded by emotion and the ghosts of the past. Maybe he should let them guide him, here.

Or maybe he was just making excuses to himself, looking for reasons why he should let her back into his life. Because, damn it to hell, he'd missed her, and seeing her again made him realise what a huge hole she'd left in his life. A hole he'd told himself was filled perfectly adequately by work, and now he knew for certain that he'd been lying to himself all along.

'What's it going to be, Xav?' she asked softly.

Knowing that he was probably making a huge mistake, he nodded. 'I'll print out the papers for you now. Read through them, call me if you have questions, and we'll see what you come up with.'

'Thank you.' She paused. 'You won't regret this.'

He'd reserve judgement on that until he'd seen her in action. 'It's two months until harvest. Let's use it as a trial. If we can work together, then fine. If we can't, then you sell your half of the vineyard to me. Deal?'

'So you're expecting me to prove myself to you?' Her eyes widened. 'Even though I own half the vineyard?'

'I'm saying that I don't know if we can work with each other,' Xavier said. 'Look, if you took a job somewhere, you'd have a trial period to see if you and the new company suited each other. This is no different.'

'And if it doesn't work out, I'm the one who has to walk away? I'm the one who loses?'

'My roots are here,' he said simply. 'Would you rip me from them?'

She was silent for a long, long time. And then she stood up and held out her hand. 'Two months, and then we'll discuss our options. Including the possibility of me selling to you, but also including the possibility of dissolving the partnership and me keeping my part of the vineyard.'

Xavier wasn't sure whether he wanted to shake her for being obstinate, or admire her backbone. In the end, he stood up, too, and took her hand.

And the feel of her skin against his took him straight back to the days when he'd driven her to all the beauty spots in the region, and they'd wandered round, hand in hand, admiring the views. Days when the summer seemed endless, the sky was always blue, and the only time he'd stopped smiling was when his mouth was busy exploring Allegra's body.

It would be so, so easy to walk round the table, draw her back into his arms and kiss her until they were both dizzy. And it would be so, so stupid. If they were going to have a chance of making this business work, she needed to be off limits.

He went through the motions of a formal handshake, then released her hand. 'We should perhaps drink to that.'

'I can't. I'm driving.'

'And I'm working in the fields this afternoon. So let's improvise.' He raised his cup of coffee. 'To Les Trois Closes.'

She clinked her cup against his. 'Les Trois Closes. And an equal partnership.'

CHAPTER THREE

ALLEGRA spent the rest of Saturday afternoon looking through the papers Xavier had printed off for her, checking things on the Internet and making notes. He'd given her his mobile number, but not his email address, and she could hardly text him a report—not if she wanted to include charts or drawings.

She sent him a quick text. *Off to London tomorrow. Back Tues, maybe Weds. Will email report, but need address. AB*

It was late evening before he replied—very briefly and to the point. Xavier had clearly turned into a man who didn't waste words; she made a mental note to keep her report extremely brief, with information in the papers behind it to support her arguments.

And she was going to be seriously busy for the next few days, sorting out loose ends in London as well as coming up with some ideas to convince Xavier that she could give something back to the vineyard.

She smiled wryly. So much for telling him that she had nothing to prove. They both knew that she did. To herself as well as to him.

'Sorry, Guy. I'm just not hungry.' Xavier eyed the slightly dried-up *cassoulet* and pushed his plate away.

'If you'd come back from the fields when I called your cellphone the first time, it might've been edible,' Guy pointed out.

'Sorry.'

'So what is it? A problem with the vines?'

'No.'

'Your biggest customer's just gone under, owing you a huge amount of money?'

Xavier shook his head impatiently. 'No. Everything's fine.'

'When you work yourself into exhaustion and you've still got shadows under your eyes because you can't sleep, everything's not fine.' Guy folded his arms and regarded his brother sternly. 'I'm not a child any more, Xav. You don't have to protect me, the way you and Papa did when we had two bad harvests on the trot and the bank wouldn't extend the vineyard's credit.'

When life as he knew it had imploded. 'I know. I'm sorry. I'm not trying to baby you.'

'If it's money, maybe I can help. The perfume house is doing OK right now. I can lend you enough to get you out of a hole—just as you helped me out a couple of years back.'

When Guy's ex-wife had cleaned him out and he'd almost had to sell his share of the perfume house. Xavier gave him a weary smile. 'Thanks, *mon frère*. It's good of you to offer. But there's no need. The vineyard's on an even keel financially, and I'm being careful about credit—even with my oldest customers.'

'Then it's Allie.'

Yeah. He couldn't think straight now she was back. 'Of course not. I'm fine,' he lied.

'You waited just a little too long before you denied it,' Guy said. 'You never really got over her, did you?'

Xavier shrugged. 'I dated.'

'But you've never let any of your girlfriends close to you—not the way you were with Allie that summer.'

'It was a long time ago, Guy. We've both grown up. Changed. We want different things out of life.'

'It sounds to me,' said Guy, 'as if you're trying to convince yourself.'

He was. Worse, he knew that he was failing. 'It's just the surprise of seeing her again. Let's drop this, Guy. I don't want to discuss it.'

'OK, I'll back off,' Guy said. 'But if you decide you do want to talk about it, you know where I am.' He patted Xavier's shoulder, then topped up their glasses. 'Just as you were there for me when it all went wrong with Véra.'

Long nights when Guy had ranted and Xavier had listened without judging.

'Maybe Lefèvre men just aren't good at picking the right women,' Xavier said. 'Papa, you, me—we've all made a mess of it.'

'Maybe.' Guy shrugged. 'Or maybe you and I just haven't met the right ones yet.'

Allegra had been the right one for him, Xavier thought. The problem was, he hadn't been the right one for her. And he needed to remember that, if he was to have any hope of a decent working relationship with her.

In London, Allegra didn't have a minute to breathe. Between sorting out a marketing plan for the vineyard; offering the lease of her flat to Gina, her best friend at the agency; sorting out what she wanted to take to France immediately and what could stay until she'd decided what she needed at the farmhouse; picking up her things from the office and trying not to bawl her eyes out when Gina threw a surprise leaving party for her and the whole of the office turned up except for her much-loathed ex-boss… There just wasn't a spare second to think about Xavier.

Until she was on the train from London to Avignon. That gave her seven hours to think about him, and to fume over the fact that he hadn't even acknowledged the receipt of her proposals, let alone asked her when she was coming back.

Getting angry and stressing about it wasn't a productive use of her time; instead, she mocked up the content for her proposed changes to the vineyard's website and a running feature about being a rookie vigneronne. But when she arrived at the TGV station, prepared to find a taxi to take her to the old central station to catch the local train through to the Ardèche, she was surprised to see Xavier leaning against the wall.

Though she wasn't surprised to see that he was attracting glances from every female in the place. Even when he was scruffy from working on the fields, he was a beautiful man. Today, he was dressed simply in black trousers and a white shirt, with an open collar and his cuffs rolled back slightly; his shoes were perfectly shined, too, she noticed, and he looked more like a model for an aftershave ad than a hotshot businessman.

He seemed to be scanning the crowds, waiting for someone. When he saw her, he lifted a hand in acknowledgement before coming to meet her.

He was waiting for *her*?

She set her cases down. 'What are you doing here?'

'Hello to you, too.'

'*Bonjour*, Monsieur Lefèvre,' she chorused dutifully. 'Seriously, what are you doing here?'

'I had business in Avignon and you need a lift back to Les Trois Closes. So it seemed sensible for me to wait for you.'

Served her right for thinking, just for one second, that Xav might've made a special trip to Avignon to pick her up. Of course not. He'd admitted to working crazy hours, and he certainly wouldn't let up the pace for her. This was the man who'd pushed her away and broken her heart. He hadn't wanted her then, and he didn't want her now. 'Thank you. How did you know I was going to be here?'

'Hortense told me.'

Allegra blinked.

Xavier shrugged. 'Now, are you going to stand there and argue all day, or can we go?' He lifted her suitcases.

'I can handle them myself,' she protested.

He shot her a look. 'Men in London might no longer have manners, but this is France.'

She subsided. 'Thank you.'

Another Gallic shrug. '*Ça ne fait rien.* How was London?'

'Fine.'

'And this is all you've brought with you?'

'I put some of my things in storage.'

'In case it doesn't work out here.' He nodded. 'It's sensible to play it safe.'

It sounded like a compliment, yet it felt like an insult. She decided not to rise to the bait. 'Did you get the proposals I emailed you?'

'Yes.'

'And?'

'I'm thinking about it.'

In other words, he was going to be difficu̵ was your business meeting?' she asked.

'Fine, thank you.'

She coughed. '*Vineyard* business, would that be?'

'No, actually.'

Infuriating man. Would it really kill him to tell her?

As if he read her mind, he smiled. 'All right, if you must know, I bunked off for the afternoon and had lunch with Marc.'

'Marc, as in Monsieur Robert? Harry's—*my* lawyer?' she corrected herself.

'We didn't discuss *you*,' he told her loftily.

She scowled. 'You know, sometimes you can be so obnoxious.'

'No, really?' He slanted her a look as he put her cases into the back of his four-wheel drive. There was the tiniest, tiniest quirk to his lips, a hint of mischief in his eyes—just like the Xav she remembered from years ago, rather than the wary stranger he'd become—and suddenly she found herself smiling back.

'Welcome back to France. Come on, I'll drive you home,' he said.

Home. Was he being polite, or did he mean it? She wasn't sure.

'What happened to your sports car?' she asked as she climbed into the passenger seat. The one his father had bought him for passing his driving test, an ancient classic car with a soft top. The one in which he'd driven her all round the Ardèche, showing her all the beauty spots—from the natural wonder of the Pont d'Arc, a huge stone arch across the Ardèche river, through to the Chauvet Grotto with its incredible thirty-thousand-year-old cave paintings, and the beautiful lake in an old volcano crater at Issarles.

'It wasn't practical,' he said, surprising her. 'This is.'

'Practical?' She didn't follow. Practical had never been a consideration. Xav had loved that car. He'd chosen it in favour of a new one, and restored it with the help of Michel, who owned the garage in the village and had sighed with Xavier over how beautiful the car was. She and Guy had teased him mercilessly about the amount of attention he gave the car, but he'd never risen to the bait. He'd simply smiled and polished the chrome a little bit more.

'Sometimes I need to use my car off road, and sometimes I need to take a few cases of wine to a customer.'

'This has rather expensive upholstery for a delivery van,' she remarked.

'What do you expect me to do, use a pushbike and trailer?'

She had a vision of him doing just that and smiled. 'Well, hey, that'd be the eco way of doing things.'

'This car is as eco as a four-wheel drive gets, right now.'

'This is an eco car?' she asked, surprised.

'It's a hybrid,' he explained. 'I put my money where my mouth is. The vineyard's organic. I carry the ethos through to the rest of my life, too.'

A life she'd once thought to share. A life she knew nothing about.

Not that she wanted to tell him that, so she subsided and looked out at the countryside as Xavier drove, the fields full of sunflowers and lavender becoming hillier and full of vines and chestnut trees as they travelled deeper into the Ardèche.

Two suitcases really weren't much. Xavier knew women who needed more than that for a week's holiday, and Allegra was supposed to be here for the next two months. Was she going back to London again to bring more things over, or had she arranged to have things shipped? Or wasn't she planning to stay? 'What are you going to do about transport while you are over here?' he asked.

'I assume Harry still has his 2CV. I'll get that insured for me to drive.'

Harry's old banger? She had to be joking. 'He hasn't used it for years. You'll need to get a mechanic to look at it and check it over before you drive it—that's if it's still driveable.' He gave her an enquiring glance. 'Why didn't you bring your car over from England?'

'I don't have a car. I don't need one in London; I use public transport,' she explained.

'What if you had to go away?'

'If it was on company business, I used a hire car.'

Knowing that it was none of his business, and yet unable to leave it alone, he asked, 'So why did you resign? Why not just take a sabbatical?'

'I don't think the MD would have been too keen on that.'

'Your boss?'

Her lip curled. 'For the last six months, anyway.'

'You worked elsewhere before then?'

'No.' She sighed. 'Peter took over the agency, about a week after my boss—the Head of Creative—went on sick leave. I was Acting Head in his absence.'

'And now your boss is back?'

'He didn't come back,' Allegra said softly. 'He decided it was too much stress, so he took early retirement, two months ago.'

'And you took his place?'

'That was the idea. But Peter brought someone else in. Clearly he'd been planning it for a while.'

Her words were cool and calm, but he could hear the hurt in her voice. In her position, he would've been furious: doing a job for months, on a promise that it would be his, and then having it snatched away. Why hadn't Allegra fought back? 'Peter being this MD?'

She nodded.

The expression on her face told him more. 'He was the one who made you go to New York before Harry's funeral.' It was a statement rather than a question.

She swallowed. 'He said I had to prove myself to the company.'

'But you'd been Acting Head for...?' He paused for her answer.

'Five months.'

'So you'd already proved that you could do the job.'

She shrugged. 'That wasn't how he saw it. And he's the MD. What he says, goes.'

'And everyone else in the agency gets on with him?'

'No, but they put up with him. It's not exactly easy to change jobs in the current economic climate.'

'So if Harry hadn't left you the vineyard, what would you have done?' Xavier asked, curious.

'Probably found myself another job. And worked out where I could get a reference.'

Xavier blinked. 'He refused to give you a reference?'

'Not *refused*, exactly. But he could have written a reference that would've made any prospective employer have second thoughts about me.'

'Then you could have sued him for defamation.'

'Mud sticks,' she said. 'And would you employ someone who'd sued her previous employer? Doesn't that just scream "troublemaker" at you?'

'You have a point,' he said.

'I might've gone freelance, worked for myself. This just crystallised it for me—it was time to get out.'

So she *was* running from her job. That didn't bode too well for her working at the vineyard. He'd wondered before what would happen when the going got too tough for her; now, he was pretty sure she'd do exactly what his mother had done. Walk out. Find someone to rescue her.

Just as she was obviously seeing the vineyard as a way of rescuing her from the collapse of her job in London.

'If you sold the vineyard to me, it would give you enough money to set yourself up in business,' he pointed out quietly. 'You could go and do what you really want to do in London, instead of being stuck here.'

'I'm not selling, Xav. I'm going to make this work.' She lifted her chin. 'And I'm not going to let you bully me into changing my mind.'

Bully her? He stared at her in surprise for a moment before concentrating on the road again. 'I wouldn't bully you.'

'Intimidate, then.'

'I'm not intimidating.'

'Actually, you are,' she said quietly. 'You have strong views and you're not afraid to voice them.'

'Which doesn't make me a bully. I do listen. I listened to you, the other day,' he reminded her. 'Without judging. Much,' he added belatedly, trying to be fair.

'And you're so sure of yourself, of where you're going.'

'I see what needs to be done, and I do it without making a drama out of it.' He shrugged. 'If that's intimidating…sorry. It's how I am.'

'Whatever you throw at me, I'll handle it.'

So there was still some fire there, even if it was buried fairly deeply right now. 'Is that a challenge?' he asked, interested.

'No,' she said, sounding bone-deep tired. 'Why do men always have to make issues out of things?'

'I'm not making an issue out of things. Yes, I admit, I'd prefer you to be a silent partner, the way Harry was, but that obviously isn't going to happen. For the next two months, we're stuck with each other. I'll expect a lot from you, but I won't go out of my way to make life difficult for you.'

'Thank you for that. And I do mean to pull my weight. I'm not a slacker.'

Had this Peter accused her of that? he wondered. But for her to have wrapped up all the loose ends in London over the last couple of days and said her goodbyes, as well as emailing him a detailed report that had clearly taken time to research—no, Allegra Beauchamp wasn't a slacker.

Finally, Xavier parked on the gravel outside Harry's farmhouse. He was out of the car and holding the door open for Allegra before she had a chance to unclip her seat belt, and then he took her cases from the back of his car.

'Thank you,' she said. 'Um, would you like to come in for a coffee or something?'

'It's kind of you to ask, but I have work to do.'

'Of course.' And there was something else she needed to know. Her normal skill with words deserted her, and she ended up blurting out, 'Um, is it going to be a problem for your wife, having me as your business partner?'

Xavier gave her a speaking look. 'If you want to know if I'm married, *chérie*, just ask me—don't do that feminine subterfuge stuff. It's annoying.'

She felt the colour flood into her face. 'All right. Are you married?'

'No. Happy?'

Right at that moment, she really regretted accepting the lift from him. 'It doesn't actually make a difference to me whether you're married or not,' she said, looking him straight in the eye. 'I was just thinking, if you were involved with someone, I'd like to reassure her that I'm no threat to your relationship. Out of courtesy to her.'

Xavier spread his hands. 'You wouldn't be a threat.'

Of course not—he'd made it clear years ago that she wasn't what he was looking for. That he didn't have time for her. Though the comment still stung.

It must have shown in her face, because he said, this time a little more gently, 'I'm not involved with anyone. My energy's concentrated on the vineyard. I don't have time for complications.'

'Don't tell me you're celibate.' The words were out before she could stop them.

He raised an eyebrow. 'Asking about my sex life now, Allegra?'

This time, her blush felt even deeper. 'No. I didn't mean to say that aloud. And it was intrusive. I apologise.'

'But you asked, so you clearly want to know.'

'Forget it.'

His smile had a definite edge. 'No, I'm not celibate. I like sex. A lot, if you remember.'

Oh, God, yes. She remembered. And nobody had ever made her feel the way Xav had made her feel. As if she were drowning in pure pleasure.

There was a glint in his eye. 'But, as I said, I don't have time for complications.'

'You've changed a lot in ten years.'

'So have you. Let's leave it that we're both older and wiser.'

'Yes. Thank you for the lift, Monsieur Lefèvre,' she said politely, and picked up her cases.

She heard the sound of his car moving away on the gravel as she opened the front door, and sighed inwardly. So much for being business partners. He hadn't even wanted to discuss her proposals.

She greeted Hortense and took her cases upstairs. While she was unpacking, her phone bleeped. She glanced at the screen, surprised to see that the text was from Xavier. *See you in the office at midday tomorrow. Bring a loaf of white bread.*

It was an odd request, but at least it showed that he was prepared to talk to her about the business. And maybe the bread was meant to be her share of lunch. She finished unpacking before asking Hortense for the keys to Harry's old 2CV.

It was parked neatly in the barn Harry used as a garage. How many times had he picked her up in this from the station in Avignon? It looked cramped and old-fashioned, compared to Xav's sleek grey four-wheel drive, but it was still transport. If it was good enough for Harry, it was good enough for her.

She turned the key in the ignition, but the engine refused to start. It was pointless pulling up the bonnet and looking at the engine, because she knew next to nothing about how they worked; Xavier was right, she'd have to ask Michel—if he was still the local mechanic—to tow it in and inspect it. In the meantime, what? Given that she'd only be going to the village or over to the chateau, hiring a car seemed a bit over the top.

Then she saw the ancient bicycle leaning against the wall.

A quick check of the tyres told her that it was in working order. She experimented by cycling round the yard, testing that the brakes and gears worked. Well, she only needed transport for one. This would do her fine for the next couple of months. If she needed to go farther afield than the village or the vineyard office, she could use the train. And this was definitely a good way to help her get fit. There was even a wicker basket on the front of the bike that was big enough to carry her laptop and a handbag.

Perfect.

And tomorrow was the real beginning of her new life.

CHAPTER FOUR

THE next morning, Allegra cycled into the village and picked up a loaf from the *boulangerie* on the way to the office.

Did Xavier really think she'd be happy just to roll up at midday? No chance. They were partners, so her working day would be just as long as his. She'd told him she wasn't a slacker, and she'd prove it to him. But when she arrived at the chateau, the office block looked deserted. She tried the door: locked.

Oh, brilliant.

That left her three options. She could disturb Guy and ask if he had a spare key—though, as he'd already told her that the vineyard was Xavier's department, he probably wouldn't have one. She could ring Xavier's mobile and ask him to bring the key down—and risk annoying him if he was in the middle of something important. Or, given that she'd charged up her laptop the previous evening, she could find herself a comfortable spot in the gardens and work in the sunshine.

It was a no-brainer, really.

She took her laptop case out of the basket and propped her bike against the wall. There was a large chestnut tree to the side of the office block; she settled herself next to it, leaning back against the trunk, and powered up her laptop. The spot really was idyllic, she thought; she could smell the roses and the lavender, and hear the drowsy hum of the bees on their quest for pollen. Given the choice between this and her desk in a busy London office block, where all she could see from the windows were more office blocks, she knew where she'd rather be right now.

At quarter to twelve, Xavier parked outside the office, then slammed his car door and strode over to her. 'What do you think you are doing?' he asked.

'Working.'

'In the garden?'

She gave him her sweetest smile. 'As my business partner hasn't given me a set of keys to our office, yet, and the door's locked—yes.'

He frowned. 'Harry didn't have an office here.'

'I'm not Harry—and I'm not cycling from my house to yours every time I need a piece of paper. Just so you know, I'll be working here in office hours.'

He folded his arms. 'There isn't a spare office for you to use.'

Oh, wasn't there? 'I seem to remember seeing one on Saturday.'

'That's my secretary's office.'

It sounded plausible, but there was one huge hole in that theory. 'So why isn't she here now?'

'She's on a week's leave. Her daughter's just had a baby and she needs to be there to help.'

Allegra liked the fact he seemed relaxed about his secretary having time off for something so important. But it still left questions. 'Why don't you have a temp in while she's away?'

'Because Thérèse doesn't like people touching her paperwork. So don't even *think* about suggesting you can use her desk while she's away.'

Since when would a powerhouse like Xavier Lefèvre let anyone tell him what to do? She couldn't stop a gurgle of laughter escaping.

'Why are you laughing?' he asked.

'At the thought of someone bossing you about. Your secretary must be seriously scary.'

He rolled his eyes. 'Thérèse doesn't boss me about. And she happens to be extremely good at organising things.'

'I'll take your word for it.' She gave him another sweet smile. 'I take it you've been in the fields this morning? And you'll be there later this afternoon?'

'Yes.'

'Then your desk is free most of the day. Good. I can work there while you're in the fields. Unless you want me to work in the fields with you,' she added, 'in which case a chair in your office will do just fine during our admin period—the middle of the day, I believe you said? It won't take long to add my laptop to your network.'

He stared at her, his expression a mixture of admiration and annoyance. 'You've got it all planned, haven't you?'

'Yup.'

'You're difficult.'

She laughed. 'Pots and kettles.'

'La pelle se moque du fourgon,' he shot back.

'What?'

'"The shovel mocks the poker",' he translated. 'As we say in France. Same thing.'

She rolled her eyes. 'You always have to have the last word, don't you?'

He gave her another of those smiles she remembered from the station: full of mischief, slightly self-mocking, and utterly irresistible. 'Yes. Did you bring the bread?'

'*Voilà.*' She indicated the loaf in her bicycle's pannier. 'I assume it's my contribution to lunch?'

'No.' He unlocked the office door and shepherded her inside. 'Excuse me. I'm filthy. I had intended at least to have clean hands before you turned up.' He headed to the kitchen and washed his hands thoroughly, then took a platter from the fridge. 'Lunch today is cold meat and salad.'

'I don't expect you to provide lunch for me every day, Xav.' She used the pet form of his name without even thinking about it. 'I can bring a sandwich with me.'

'As you wish.' He spread his hands. 'But we're having a working lunch today, so you might as well share this with me. I see you cycled in.'

She nodded. 'You were right about Harry's 2CV. I couldn't even get it to start. Hortense is going to chat to the local garage for me and see if they can get it going again.'

'I could lend you a car.'

Did he think she was fishing? Wrong, wrong, wrong. And she wanted to prove to him that she could stand on her own two feet perfectly well—that she wouldn't be a burden. 'No need,' she said brightly. 'I'm fine with Harry's old bicycle.'

He raised an eyebrow. 'Even if it rains?'

'I'll just make sure my laptop's in a waterproof bag. Or I can use your computer while you're getting soaked in the fields, and copy it to a memory stick or email it to myself at the end of the day.'

'Stubborn, aren't you?'

'*La pelle se moque du fourgon,*' she threw back at him.

'Now that's cheeky.' But he looked amused rather than annoyed. 'Here.' He fished in his pocket, removed a key from his key ring and tossed it to her. 'Don't lose it.'

She caught it deftly, took her own key ring from her handbag and slid the office key onto it. 'I won't. Is there an alarm code?'

'Yes. Harry's birthday.'

Was he testing her, to see that she did actually know the date? Well, she wasn't going to let him rattle her. 'That's fine. The French format's the same as English, isn't it—two-digit day, then two-digit month?'

'Yes.' He handed her the platter. 'Take this in. I'll bring everything else.'

'Do you normally eat at your desk?' she asked, when he came in carrying the crockery, cutlery, a cobblestone-shaped loaf studded with olives that she recognised as *pavé*, Harry's favourite, and two glasses of iced water.

'It's convenient. And don't start. I bet you usually do the same.'

'Well, yes,' she admitted.

'Right. Help yourself.'

'Thank you.' She paused. 'As this is a working lunch, can we start with the website? I take it you got the recommendations I sent you?'

'Yes.'

His face was expressionless, but the fact that he didn't sound enthusiastic wasn't promising. 'What did you think?' she asked.

'Do you have to go into the heritage stuff?'

She frowned. 'Xav, it's a strength of the vineyard, and we should make the most of it. Your family has grown grapes here for years and years. If you'd tell me when they actually started, there might be an anniversary coming up that we could use to—'

'I don't think we should be going on about the past,' he cut in.

'Why not?'

'Because we haven't always been as successful as we are now. I don't want to drag up the past—any hint of failure, even if it was years ago, could make our suppliers nervous.'

'What failure?'

'It's not important now.'

She wasn't so sure. But he'd made it clear that he wasn't going to talk about it.

'I think we should concentrate on what we do now. What we're good at.' Xavier frowned. 'To be honest, I don't think we need to do any more marketing than we do now. Our customers like what we produce. I'm not planning to buy more land and increase the quantity of our output, so what's the point in making a big fuss?'

'Do you want this vineyard to be a huge success or not?'

He rolled his eyes. 'Don't ask ridiculous questions.'

'Then you need to talk about it, Xav. Tell people what we're better at doing than other producers.'

He arched an eyebrow. 'We?'

She flushed. 'All right, so I haven't done any of the physical work for this year's crop. But I'm learning. And I intend to pull my weight, whatever you think.'

He made a non-committal noise and cut some more bread.

'Who designed the original website?' she asked, curious.

'One of Guy's business contacts.'

Guy, Xavier's younger brother, clearly worked from home but had nothing to do with the vineyard. Years ago, she remembered Guy being the scientific type; she'd always thought he'd become a doctor. Obviously he hadn't. 'What does Guy do?' she asked, helping herself to cold meat and salad and accepting the piece of bread Xavier offered her.

'He's a nose.'

'A what?'

'A parfumier. He's gifted.'

Guy made perfume?

Xavier continued. 'His degree was in chemistry, but, like me, he doesn't have time for distractions. He owns half a perfume house in Grasse and heads up the R and D arm, directing the development of new perfumes. Half the time he lives there, but he also has a lab here—he spends most weekends at the chateau, or comes here when he wants to think and work on fragrance ideas in peace and quiet without office politics getting in the way. Except in harvest, when he drives the tractor for me.'

That, she thought, explained the rose garden. Guy's raw materials. 'Your mother must enjoy trying out his creations.'

'Chantal doesn't live here,' Xavier said, his tone short and warning her not to ask further.

Allegra remembered Chantal Lefèvre as the quintessential elegant Frenchwoman—always dressed in cream or navy, her dark hair beautifully coiffed and her make-up discreet and flawless. Allegra had always felt shy and faintly scruffy in her presence. So why didn't Chantal live at the chateau now? Was it that she couldn't bear to be there without Jean-Paul?

And yet Xavier had just referred to his mother by her first name, as if she weren't actually related to him. Odd. Chantal hadn't exactly been the demonstrative type but, given her own family background, Allegra wasn't really in a position to judge Chantal's relationship with her sons. Best to leave it, she decided, and brought the conversation back to a neutral topic. 'You said yesterday that the vineyard's organic, but the website doesn't say anything about it. How long has it been organic?'

'We've been certified for the last three years. If you want to see the files to see exactly what was involved, fine—though I should warn you it's all in French.'

'My French needs brushing up,' Allegra said. 'I suppose this is as good a way as any of getting back into it.' She looked at him. 'I want to do a blog, too—about learning to be a vigneronne. In French and English. Would you mind looking over my translations for the first few, so I don't make us look stupid?'

'You're here for two months,' he said.

'During which I'm going to bring new ideas to the business,' she said. 'This is an ongoing project.'

'I see.' He looked wary.

'Xavier, I have to start somewhere.'

'Then I suggest,' Xavier said, 'we start with the product. Which is why we need the bread.'

'You've lost me.'

'Already?' He rolled his eyes. 'It's to cleanse your palate between tasting.'

'You mean we're going to taste wine?'

'*You're* going to taste wine,' he corrected. 'What wine do you normally drink in London?'

'You're not going to like this,' she warned. 'New World.'

'So do a lot of our customers, outside France,' Xavier said, seemingly unruffled. 'What's your favourite?'

'New Zealand Sauvignon Blanc.'

He nodded. 'It's a good grape. Why do you like it?'

'Because of the taste.'

He waved his hand in a circle, encouraging her to expand on her answer.

'It's fruity,' she said.

'Good. Which fruit?'

'Sorry, I don't know.'

He sighed. 'When you say fruit, do you mean lemons, gooseberries, strawberries, melon, blackcurrants?'

She was pretty sure that a white wine wasn't supposed to taste of blackcurrants. 'Gooseberries. Is that right?'

'There isn't a right or wrong answer,' he said, surprising her. 'But in a good New Zealand Sauvignon Blanc, I'd expect gooseberries, maybe a hint of melon and citrus. Some are complex, some aren't. It depends on a lot of things. So your first lesson today is that the way the grape tastes has a lot to do with the winemaker—but it also has a lot to do with the *terroir*, the soil it's grown in.' A tiny furrow appeared between his eyebrows. 'Harry must've taught you this?'

'Sort of. I didn't pay as much attention as I should,' Allegra admitted. 'Anyway, he used to water down the wine for me when I was younger.'

Xavier smiled. 'You water it down for the children so they grow up appreciating it—and when they're eighteen they're less likely to go and binge on the stuff.'

She remembered.

'Here in the south, the kind of wines we make are probably closer to the kind of wines they make in Australia and New Zealand.'

'And we produce mainly rosé and white here, yes?'

'Yes. The rosé's *vin de pays*, also known as "country wine", which is a step above table wine. And the best is AOC—*appellation d'origine contrôlée*.'

He actually looked approving, and her heartbeat quickened just a tiny bit. 'I take it you know that wine in France is labelled by the area in which it grows, not by the grape?'

'Yes, but I don't think it's that helpful to consumers. If they know they like, say, Grenache, then why not tell them it's Grenache in the bottle, the way the New World producers do, instead of making them jump through hoops to understand what's in there?'

'Fair point. And, actually, we do say on our labels. Our rosé's mainly Grenache, so it's easy drinking—chill it down to four degrees and it's perfect for lazy summer afternoons.'

He spread his hands. 'I can talk all day but you're only going to learn if you experience it. Which is what we're going to do when we've finished lunch.'

'Why does this feel like taking my driving test?' she asked wryly.

He shrugged. 'It's not a big deal, Allie. It's just setting a baseline. If I'm to teach you what I know, I need to know what you know already so we don't repeat stuff you don't need to go over.'

A tiny frisson shimmered up her spine. He'd slipped back into calling her by her old pet name. And the last time Xavier had taught her something...

She shook herself mentally. That summer was in the past, and staying there. They hadn't talked about it, but they didn't need to: they were both older and wiser, and they weren't going to repeat their mistakes. So there was no point in dragging up the fact that he'd pushed her away, hard enough to make her end their relationship.

This was business. 'Thank you,' she said, hoping her voice sounded steadier than it felt, and concentrated on eating her lunch.

When they'd finished, she helped Xavier take the remains into the kitchen. His desk was already practically clear; he moved his in-tray to the floor, then fished out a white tablecloth from a box underneath his desk and spread it over the wood.

'Why do you need a tablecloth?' Allegra asked.

'So you can judge the colour of the wine properly. Did Harry never do this with you?'

'Not that I can remember,' she admitted. 'We were too busy talking about other things.'

'And you've never been to a wine tasting event?'

'No—but, Xav, hang on. I'm cycling back to the *mas*. I can't drink.'

'You don't actually drink wine when you're tasting—not if you're serious about it,' he explained. 'If you glug down half a dozen glasses on the trot, you won't remember anything about what they tasted like, and that negates the point. You taste, you spit it out, you make notes, and then you cleanse your palate with water and white bread before you try the next one.'

Enlightenment dawned. 'So *that's* why you wanted the bread.'

'*Exactement.*' He took a bottle from another box under his desk and handed it to her.

It was perfectly chilled.

'You use a screw-cap, like the New World producers?'

'For the *vin de pays*, yes. I'd rather have screw-tops than plastic corks because you don't have landfill issues. But for the AOC I use cork—it helps the wine age better, it's a renewable resource and it's biodegradable.'

Xav clearly thought deeply about what he did and its effect on the world; he'd grown up to become a man with integrity.

Pity he hadn't been so thoughtful ten years ago.

He took the bottle back from her. 'I was going to let you read the label,' he said, 'but I don't want to put ideas in your head. I want your gut reaction to the wine.'

He unscrewed the cap and poured her about a third of a glassful. 'This is a tasting serve. This means there's lots of space in the glass so you can swirl the wine around and test the aroma, and also so you have a chance to see the colour.' He tilted the glass over the tablecloth. 'Like this—you need to look at the colour of the body of the wine and the rim.'

She knew she was supposed to be looking at the wine. But she couldn't help looking at Xavier's hands. Strong, capable and slightly roughened by work, they were the hands of a man who saw what needed to be done and did it, not someone who left things to other people. And yet she knew his fingers could be infinitely gentle, too. Sensual. They'd teased a response from her body that she'd never quite managed with anyone else.

'Allegra?'

'Sorry. I was miles away.'

'If you'd rather not do this, it isn't a problem.'

'It's not that.' Though she'd rather dance barefoot across hot coals than tell him what she'd been thinking about. 'You were saying—the colour of the body and the rim.'

'The wine should look clear.'

'It's not as dark as I expected,' she said. 'It's almost pale peach. I thought rosés were pinker than that.' As pink as her cheeks felt, right at that moment.

'It depends on the grape you use and how it's produced. And the blend. Now, you swirl the wine in the glass. This mixes oxygen with the wine and releases the aroma. Your first sniff should be with caution—if it smells burnt, there's too much sulphite. Then do it again, this time with concentration—you're looking to see what aromas you get and the intensity.'

He passed the glass to her and she nearly dropped it when his fingers brushed lightly against hers.

This was crazy.

She'd been over Xavier for years. And she couldn't afford to fall for him again, not now they were business partners. That would be a huge, huge complication; he'd already warned her that he had no time for complications. Neither did she. He was *off limits*.

'So what can you smell?' he asked.

Right at that moment, Xavier reminded her of his younger brother, all intense and serious. She couldn't resist the urge to tease him slightly. She batted her eyelashes at him. 'Fruit?'

'Can you be a bit more specif—? Oh.' He rolled his eyes.

She grinned. 'Gotcha.'

'Very funny.' But then his eyes were smiling right back at her. Warm and sexy and utterly irresistible, and she was seriously glad she was sitting down because her knees turned straight to jelly.

'Cranberries,' she said. 'That's what it smells like. Fruity but dry.'

'Taste it.'

There was just a hint of an accent in his deep voice, and the way he spoke the phrase made her look straight at his mouth. Bad move, because he had a beautiful mouth, with even white teeth and a full lower lip. She could remember just how it had tasted against hers; and how easy it would be to brush her mouth against his, nibbling his lower lip until he opened his mouth to let her explore him.

'You need to swish the wine round your mouth, because different parts of your mouth detect different kinds of tastes,' he told her. 'At the back of tongue, it's bitter. The side is sour. The centre is salt and the front is sweet. Your gums react to the tannin in wine—it makes them feel dry.'

Her mouth felt dry, right now, and she could feel her lips parting. She only hoped that Xavier assumed she was about to taste the wine, not thinking about tasting him. Or was this his way of teasing her back?

'Roll it around your mouth,' he said. 'Think about the body.'

The body of the wine. Not his body. Not about how he'd broadened out, or how powerful his shoulders were now, or wondering whether his skin would still feel the same against her hands.

'The body's how heavy it feels on your tongue,' he added.

He probably meant to be helpful, but it just made things worse. It made her think of the way he used to kiss her, demanding and yet giving at the same time. His tongue teasing hers. His lips coaxing a response.

And she swallowed the wine, completely involuntarily.

Oh, hell. How to make herself look like an idiot. He'd specifically told her not to swallow. She was supposed to be thinking about the wine. But how could she when her head was full of him? How he'd tasted when he'd kissed her, all those years ago... Like the ginger chocolates he favoured, dark and hot and intense.

'Sorry. I, um…made a hash of that.'

'It's OK. Just think about the wine and how long it lingers afterwards—that's the finish. The longer the finish, the better the wine. Does it make you want another taste, or is it too bitter, too sour, not the kind of taste you enjoy?'

'It tastes of berries,' she said. 'Cranberries, raspberries. Maybe peaches, or maybe I'm letting the colour influence me.'

'And the finish?'

It was pointless in bluffing, so she went for honesty. 'I'm not sure,' she said. 'It's not something I've ever really paid attention to before. Can I use this one as a benchmark, and tell you when I've tried another?'

He looked approving. 'That's good—you think logically. Write down your thoughts, then we'll do the next one—and we'll compare what you found with what it says on the label later.' He took another bottle from under his desk, brought out a corkscrew from the drawer, and opened the bottle effortlessly.

'This one's a bit unusual because it's completely Viognier, though I have thought about mixing some Rolle with it and I'm planning to experiment with a blend, this harvest.'

She bit her lip. 'I'm sorry, you're going to think me completely hopeless—but I haven't heard of Viognier or Rolle.'

'Viognier has been neglected for a while, but it's becoming fashionable again,' Xavier said. 'It's one of the older varieties of grapes—it's been grown in Provence since Roman times, maybe even before that. Rolle's another very old variety. I'm growing it in a quiet corner of the vineyard for an experiment.' He poured her a tasting serve. 'Tell me what you see.'

'It's very pale gold—there's almost a green tinge at the rim.' She swirled the wine, then sniffed. 'No burning smell.' She sniffed again. 'You're going to think I'm crazy. It smells of flowers to me.' And one in particular. 'Honeysuckle.'

'I think,' he said, 'you might be a natural at this. Anything else?'

'Pears, I think.' She took a mouthful, let it swoosh over her tongue, then spat it out. 'It tastes of melon and peaches, and it makes my tongue tingle. It's definitely dry—and the finish is longer than the rosé's, though I think I'd prefer the rosé for the garden on a summer afternoon.'

Either she'd been playing him for a fool earlier or she was a quick learner.

Given what he remembered of her, Xavier was pretty sure that it was the latter.

And he really, really had to stop thinking of that summer. Had to stop looking at her mouth and wondering what it would be like to kiss her now.

He had no idea what possessed him to uncork a bottle of Clos Quatre. His baby. But, before he knew it, he'd poured her a tasting serve of the wine.

Her eyes met his. Saw the challenge. Answered it.

And then she picked up the glass. Surveyed it critically.

'It looks like rubies.'

One sniff. A second. 'Berries—but darker than raspberries. Blackberries, maybe, and something else I can't work out. Herby?'

'That'd be the *garrigue*. The scent of scrubland on limestone soil,' he explained.

And then she sipped.

He couldn't help watching her mouth. A perfect rose-bud. She'd moistened her lips slightly before she'd tasted the wine, and the sunlight glinted on the sheen of her mouth.

Did she have any idea how alluring she was?

And it wasn't from make-up, either. Today, Allegra was dressed far more practically; rather than trying to cycle here in a business suit and heels, she was wearing flat, sensible shoes and soft, pale denim teamed with a short-sleeved T-shirt. She was the girl next door and she was dressed like it.

And yet she didn't look like *just* the girl next door.

Something about her kicked his heart rate up a notch.

'Blackberries,' she said.

'Hmm?' He wasn't following. At all.

'It tastes of blackberries,' she said.

And her lips were parted. Sweet and soft and inviting. With the tiniest, tiniest gloss of wine along her lower lip. Just as she'd been when she'd been eighteen and they'd taken a bottle to drink in the evening by the lake.

He couldn't resist any longer. He simply dipped his head and kissed her, touching the tip of his tongue to the spot of wine on her lip. 'You're right. Blackberries.'

Her pupils were huge, and she looked as lost as he felt right at that moment. And then she placed her palm gently against his cheek and stroked his lower lip with the pad of her thumb. Such a light, light touch, but it made his knees buckle and his mouth open. He nibbled her thumb, keeping the touch as light as gossamer.

He wasn't sure which of them moved first, but then she was in his arms, his mouth was jammed over hers, and he was kissing her. And she was kissing him back as though she'd missed him as much as he'd missed her, was as desperate for him as he was for her. Hot and open-mouthed and demanding, yet giving and promising at the same time. His arms were wrapped tightly round her, hers were just as tightly round his, and at some point he'd sat down and pulled her with him so she was straddling his lap.

When she rocked ever so slightly against him, nudging against his erection, it made him gasp into her mouth.

Dieu, he wanted her so badly.

And they really shouldn't be doing this.

He broke the kiss. 'This is a seriously bad idea.' His head knew that. But his body wasn't listening; for the life of him, he couldn't loosen his arms from round her. And hers were wrapped just as tightly round him.

He tried again. 'We know it doesn't work between us.'

'Uh-huh. But I can't move, Xav, because you're still holding me.' Her voice was breathy, her pupils were huge and her mouth was reddened and swollen from his kisses.

And he wanted to kiss her again.

Desperately.

'*You're* still holding *me*,' he pointed out. 'Allie, we have to stop this. How the hell are we going to be able to w—?'

She brushed her mouth against his, stopping the sentence and scrambling his thoughts, and he groaned. 'I can still taste the wine on your mouth.'

'All I can taste is you.' She did it again, taking her time about it and blowing his mind in the process.

If she hadn't realised how turned on he was before, he thought wryly, she'd be in no doubt of it now. He was as hard as iron. And it would take him all of five seconds to strip her naked and bury himself inside her.

With a huge effort, he shrugged free of her embrace, dropped his hands to her waist, and lifted her off his lap. 'We're not doing this.'

'Pushing me away again, Xav?' There was a hint of bitterness in her smile.

Again? What was she talking about? He frowned. 'I've never pushed you away.'

She scoffed. 'You know damn well you have.'

Was she talking about their break-up? Blaming him for it? He felt his eyes narrow. 'You were the one who called a halt.'

'Because you made it clear you'd had enough. That I didn't fit in to your new life.'

He stared at her. 'Did I, hell. I was there, and I remember.'

'I was there too, and *I* remember,' she countered. 'I asked you when you were coming to London. You said you were too busy.'

Yes, because everything had gone wrong at the vineyard. They'd been close to losing everything. And his mother had walked out in the middle of the chaos, leaving his father devastated. Xavier had been faced with a choice: walk away, too, and start his job in Paris, or put everything on hold and support his family. 'And you couldn't have waited a little while, until things had settled down for me?'

'What was to settle down, Xav? You already had a flat sorted out in Paris. You had a job. OK, so it might've taken you a couple of weeks to find your feet, but you...' She shook her head. 'It was obvious to me that you'd changed your mind. That I was just a—a holiday romance for you, so you were making excuses not to see me. Perhaps you'd already met someone else, but you were working up to dumping me.'

'There was never anyone else. If you'd asked me, I'd have told you that.' He blew out a breath. 'I can't believe that you had so little trust in me. And what about you? The second I didn't drop everything for you, you decided it was over.'

'I didn't expect you to drop everything for me,' she retorted. 'But it would've been nice if you'd called me, once in a while, instead of making me call you all the time.'

He felt a muscle flicker in his cheek. 'I told you, there was a lot going on.'

'And you couldn't have spared just a couple of minutes to say you were up to your eyes but you were thinking of me?'

Xavier threw his hands up in disgust. She was just like his mother, and just like Guy's ex-wife. 'What is it with women? If we're not paying you a hundred per cent attention a hundred per cent of the time…'

'I wasn't asking for *all* of your attention. Just a bit of it.' She glared at him, resting her hands on her hips. 'Talk about unreasonable.'

He scoffed. 'Says the woman who called it off.'

'You pushed me into it. I'd had enough of trailing behind you, like some pathetic doormat. So, yes, I called it off. What did you expect, that I'd trot meekly behind you and wait until you dumped me officially?'

'No. I just expected you to trust me. Clearly you didn't, so it's just as well you called it off.' He got to his feet. 'Excuse me. I have things to do in the fields.'

'Running away from the truth?'

'No. Putting space between us, before I say something we'll both regret. What happened just now was a huge mistake—and, yes, I'll take the blame for it. I can assure you that it's not going to happen again. And if you're serious about pulling your weight in the vineyard, then I suggest you work on tasting the wine, making notes and checking it against the labels instead of flirting with me.'

Her cheeks went scarlet. 'I wasn't flirting.'

No? She'd been kissing him back. Intimately. But there was no point in arguing with her. 'I'm going back to work. And you can do what the hell you like.' As long as it meant leaving him alone. 'Excuse me.' He rose from his chair, moved past her—very, very careful not to let any part of him touch any part of her—and left his office.

CHAPTER FIVE

ALLIE sat back in her chair and lifted a shaking hand to her mouth. Did Xavier really think she'd wanted them to break up?

The words of their argument echoed in her head. According to him, he hadn't pushed her away. Was it possible that she'd misinterpreted things back then?

Yet, when she'd said their relationship was over, he'd agreed. He hadn't asked her why. He'd let her go without fighting for her—and she'd assumed it was because she'd saved him the bother of ending it himself.

Then again, he'd taken the blame for that flare of passion between them just now—even though she'd been there all the way with him. He'd as good as admitted how much he wanted her. Just as she wanted him.

But he'd also made it clear he had no intention of letting it happen again.

She blew out a breath. This was a mess. And they definitely had crossed wires about what had happened all those years ago. The way he remembered it wasn't the same way that she remembered it. They needed to talk about it properly; then maybe they could work out where they were going from here.

Especially as they co-owned a vineyard. If they didn't sort it out, working together was going to be excruciating.

She tried ringing his mobile phone—but either he wasn't in a position to take the call or he wasn't in the mood for talking to her, because he didn't answer. So instead, she texted him. *Xav, I'm sorry. I don't want to fight with you. We're both older and wiser and we both want the business to succeed. We can work together.*

Provided they talked properly and cleared things up between them.

I'll see you tomorrow.

She tidied up in the office and restoppered the bottles of wine. There wasn't much more she could do here. Maybe she should take the wine back to Harry's and work on the tasting, as he'd suggested. She could send him her notes, to show that she was serious and she wasn't just playing at being a vigneronne.

And burying herself in work, giving herself something else to concentrate on, might just stop her thinking about the way he'd kissed her. The way her body had responded. The way her blood was still tingling in her veins.

She cycled home and let herself into the empty house. Although in some ways it was a relief not to have to face anyone—not when she was feeing this shaky—in other ways, she wished the housekeeper had been there. How Harry must've rattled around here on his own.

And how she wished she could change the past.

But it wasn't possible. She had to move on, not let the past drag her back.

Look at the labels, Xav had said. So she did—but not just to read the notes. This time, she looked at them with a professional eye, and she didn't like what she saw. The design of the labels just wasn't inspiring. They told the customer nothing about the wine, the vineyard—there wasn't really a brand. They simply contained the vineyard's name, the name of the wine, its classification and the year, and the fact that it was *'mis en bouteille au Domaine'*—bottled at the estate. Everything that needed to be there, without the pizzazz.

The back was a little better, telling her about the wine's bouquet and its taste. But it still had no personality. And Les Trois Closes definitely had a personality.

Letting the ideas bubble in the back of her head, she tasted the wines again, this time taking account of the notes on the label and trying to see where she agreed with them and where she couldn't pick up the scent or taste. She made notes to discuss with Xavier later, then wrote her first blog about tasting wine. Laboriously, she translated it into French and emailed the file with both the English and the French version over to Xavier.

Next, she wrote a design brief. From what Xavier had told her, she had a very clear idea of what Les Trois Closes was all about. They used traditional grapes and traditional methods, and the wine was hand crafted, so she wanted the label to reflect that. Maybe a textured label with hand-drawn lettering. It also needed a strong graphic to go with the text that legally had to be on the wine.

She sent a text to Gina. Can u do freelance job 4 me, hon? Need logo + sample wine bottle labels. Middle next week OK?xxx

Gina replied almost immediately: Sure, email brief @ home, I'll ring u if I have any queries xxx

This was a private job, not something through the agency, so it made sense to email the brief to Gina's home address rather than to work. And of course Gina would ring her with any questions: she was an excellent designer, and good at seeing to the heart of a brief, especially in cases where the client asked for one thing but clearly meant something else.

She was about to text a thank you when her phone beeped again with another text from Gina. U OK?

Far from it. She was as miserable as hell because she didn't want to be at loggerheads with Xav and she wasn't a hundred per cent sure if it was fixable, let alone how to fix it. But Gina didn't need to hear all that. Tres OK, she texted back, adding a smiley face. She emailed the brief to Gina, along with a chatty note saying how much she was enjoying it here in the Ardèche. She told her about Nicole's farm shop and café in the village, the way that the light and the air felt so different here, how fabulous the food was.

What she didn't say was that she couldn't get Xavier out of her head. Or how it could be oh so easy to be lonely, here; in London, she'd always been busy with work and had people round her, never had time to think about whether she was happy. Here, the pace of life was so much slower—and there simply weren't people around. The estate workers reported to the office at the chateau, and Hortense lived with her brother in the village. Harry had always had a basset hound; Allegra had asked Hortense what had happened to the dog and discovered that he'd been rehomed. It wouldn't be fair to bring the dog back here now. And it wouldn't be fair to buy a puppy, either, until she'd convinced Xavier that she was a worthy partner in the business.

All the same, she found herself searching the Internet, sighing over puppy pictures. Xavier didn't have a dog—at least, not that she'd seen. But if she trained her dog well, kept him under control in the fields...surely Xav wouldn't object?

Maybe she could get a rescue dog—to give an unwanted animal a second chance, just as she'd been given one.

Three clicks later, she was looking at the photograph of a dog called Beau in an Ardèchoise animal rescue centre. He was an orangey-brown-and-white dog with the most soulful brown eyes, and it was love at first sight. *Un epagneul Breton*. She grabbed her dictionary to help her with the difficult words; the more she read, the more she wanted him.

Though she could hardly collect a dog on a bicycle. And Xavier *had* offered to lend her a car...

An offer she'd refused. And an offer that might not be forthcoming again.

Half an hour later, her email pinged again. This time it was from Xavier.

I don't want to fight, either. I'm sorry, too.

Good. So let's kiss and make—oh, no. She definitely couldn't mention the *K* word. Not after the way they'd kissed each other in his office this afternoon. Especially as he'd accused her of flirting with him. She deleted the words and typed instead, Truce?

There was a long, long pause—or maybe it just felt as if time were running at a tenth of its usual speed because she so badly wanted to know how he'd react—but finally his reply came through. OK. Truce.

A few minutes later, there was another email from him: a list of Internet links for her to follow, plus a word-processed file with corrections to her French typed in red.

How to make her feel like a schoolgirl.

Then again, this wasn't about her ego. This was about their joint business, and she wanted to get this right. She'd asked for his help, and he'd given it. Besides, he hadn't just marked corrections: he'd added a couple of notes at the bottom, in English, to explain where she'd gone wrong and why.

Xavier Lefèvre would've made an excellent teacher. Then again, she thought ruefully, he would've been excellent at any job he chose. Xav wasn't one to give half measures in anything.

She heard the back door rattle; a moment later, Hortense walked into the kitchen and raised an eyebrow when she saw Allegra sitting there at her laptop.

'Sorry, will I be in your way?' Allegra asked.

Hortense shrugged. 'I can work at this end of the table.'

Allegra tidied up her notes and shoved them into a folder. 'Sorry,' she said again. This really wasn't a good state of affairs. And there was a perfectly good study next door. 'Hortense, would you mind if I go through Harry's study at the weekend?' she asked. 'I was thinking, if I put some of his things away, it would make room for mine—and I wouldn't be under your feet in here all the time.'

Hortense shrugged again. 'It's your house. Do what you will.'

'Madame Bouvier, I'm not that thick-skinned. I don't want to hurt you or ignore your feelings—but I can't keep working at the kitchen table and getting in your way.'

Her only answer was another Gallic shrug.

Allegra sighed inwardly and continued working, becoming absorbed in coding the website.

Half an hour later, Hortense put a large mug of black coffee beside her—a kind of peace offering, Allegra guessed.

'I'm off now,' Hortense announced. 'There's a casserole in the oven—*poulet Provençal*. It will be ready at seven, and there are green beans and broccoli in the fridge.'

'Thank you.' Hortense's *poulet Provençal* had always been one of Allegra's favourites: another peace offering, it seemed. And at least the housekeeper wasn't being territorial over the kitchen and insisting that Allegra didn't touch a thing—probably because she'd learned over the last few days that Allegra wasn't going to take her for granted and had washed up and put things away in the right places.

Allegra spent the evening in Harry's study, looking through his books. There were plenty on viticulture, but they were all in French. She ordered herself the English versions of the ones that looked most well thumbed; just as she finished, an email came through from Gina.

Brief looks fine. I need pics of the vineyard and surrounding area to give me some inspiration for visuals.

Well, that was something for her to do over the next few days—while she waited for Xavier to accept her new role in the business.

On the case, she emailed back.

On Friday morning, Allegra cycled into the village to pick up some bread and cheese, then cycled up to the chateau. Her heart was tattooing crazily at the thought of seeing Xavier again—and how were they going to face each other? They'd agreed to a truce, but there was still that scorching attraction between them. They were going to have to deal with that, too, and she had no idea how.

When she saw that the office block was locked, she wasn't sure if she was more disappointed or relieved. Everything was confusion where Xavier was concerned. She wanted him—and, at the same time, she wanted to be a million miles away from him.

Crazy.

She unlocked the door, then installed herself at Xavier's desk.

It was the first time she'd been in his office without him. Without his presence to command all her attention, she was able to pay more attention to her surroundings. Obviously Xavier believed in a clear-desk policy; it was a million miles away from Harry's cluttered study. And, unlike Harry, Xavier didn't keep anything personal in his workspace. This room could've belonged to anyone.

Maybe that was the way forward. Act on pure logic and keep her emotions out of this. Treat him as a client, as a business associate—and block off everything else that he'd meant to her. Pretend she didn't feel that wild surge of longing every time she looked into his eyes.

Telling herself that this was work, she booted up her laptop and got down to some work.

At quarter to twelve, Xavier parked outside the office. Allegra was clearly there; her bicycle was propped against the wall, his office window was wide open, and she'd also left the front door open—probably in the hope of cooler air circulating.

It wasn't as hot here as it was on the coast, but it was still a good deal warmer than she was used to. She'd always spent a lot of time in the pool in those long-ago summers.

And then he wished he hadn't remembered that, because his mind supplied another image. Allegra bathing naked in a mountain pool, looking like a mermaid with hair the colour of winter wheat spreading out on the surface of the water. He'd loved it when she'd worn her hair long and loose, instead of the glossy, high-maintenance style she had now.

Dieu. He really had to get himself back under control. They'd agreed to a truce—by email—and he'd promised her that he wouldn't let the events of yesterday be repeated. Even though his body was quivering with the need to touch her. He could do this. Keep it strictly business.

Maybe he needed a night out. An evening with someone who'd give and take pleasure in equal measure, and wouldn't expect anything else from him. Hot, mindless sex that would sate his body and stop his mind dwelling on Allegra Beauchamp.

Ha. Who was he trying to kid? He couldn't stop thinking about her. And making love with someone else was completely out of the question. He wouldn't be able to do it.

When he walked in though the front door, he could see her sitting at his desk. She was clearly concentrating hard on what she was doing and hadn't heard him. There was a tiny furrow between her brows; she looked serious and businesslike. And incredibly cute.

How he yearned for her.

But he'd keep himself under control. He wouldn't walk in, lift her out of his chair, take her place and settle her in his lap. Wouldn't touch his mouth to hers, coaxing and teasing until her response flared, the way it had yesterday. Instead, he walked into his office and dropped into the chair opposite the one where she was sitting—the one he reserved for clients. *'Bonjour,'* he drawled.

She looked up and her eyes widened. 'Sorry, I didn't realise you were back. I'll move. Do you always break for lunch this early?'

'At this time of year, yes. It's too hot to work outside now until later in the afternoon.'

She nodded. 'Thanks for correcting my pieces.'

'No problem.'

She gave him a cool, professional smile—though it didn't quite work. Obviously she was nervous around him. Worried that he'd kiss her again, maybe? That he'd break their truce? 'I've set up the blog now, done it in French and English and cross-referenced it, and also linked it to our website. Oh, and I looked up those links you gave me and I've ordered some books.'

'Which ones?'

She told him and he nodded. 'They're good ones to start with.'

'I'd like to take a few pictures of the vineyard. Do you have time to show me round?'

Spend more time in her company? He needed his head examined.

Not to mention a cold shower.

'Give me five minutes to have something to eat, and I'll be with you,' he said.

'It's not *that* urgent,' she said. 'I don't expect you to drop everything for me.'

She'd said something about that yesterday.

So had he been wrong, all those years ago? He certainly hadn't been thinking straight at the time, not with all the chaos going on here. Maybe he'd misunderstood her. Though he couldn't ask her straight out, not without opening a huge can of worms. He needed to think of a way of dealing with this to give minimum discomfort on both sides.

'I'm making coffee. Do you want some?'

She was clearly making an effort, so he ought to do the same. 'That'd be nice. Thanks.'

'And I bought some bread and cheese. If you'd like some?'

'Thanks. There's salad in the fridge, if you'd like to share it.'

And how much this reminded him of lunches they'd shared in the past. Picnics in a shady corner, sprawled out on a rug. He'd loved feeding her choice morsels and stealing kisses from her in between. Especially peaches. How he'd loved feeding her slices of fresh peach, and licking the juice from the corner of her mouth.

Oh, for pity's sake, could he just stop thinking about her mouth?

He waited as she saved her file and vacated his seat. But, when he sat down on the business side of his desk, his chair was still warm with her body heat. And he could smell her perfume.

How to drive a man slowly crazy...

Business, he reminded himself, and switched on his PC. It didn't take him long to find the blog she'd set up and to read through it.

He looked up from the screen as she walked back into the office with their lunch. 'You've made a good job of the blog.' And to his relief she hadn't gone on about the heritage.

She flushed. *'Merci.'*

'So you want to look round the vineyard.' He eyed her critically. 'Your shoes are sensible enough. Do you have a hat?'

She fished a baseball cap out of her laptop bag. 'Will this do?'

'Sure.' He smiled. 'It's not what I expected.'

She frowned. 'What did you expect?'

'Something floaty.' Like the straw boater she'd worn that summer, with a chiffon scarf tied round the brim and trailing down at the side.

'This is practical.'

'So I see.' He took a sip of the coffee.

Somehow they managed to get through lunch, and then he drove her over to the vines. At least driving her meant that he had to concentrate on the road.

'Is it all right for me to take pictures?' she asked when she climbed out of his car.

'Are they for the blog?'

'Yes and no,' she said. 'I want them for myself as well.'

'Any particular reason?'

'I'm a visual learner,' she explained. 'You know the old saying, "I hear and I forget, I see and I remember, I do and I understand"? Well, I see and I understand.'

Visual.

Oh, *Dieu*. How was he going to keep his mind on business instead of remembering what she looked like naked?

Tell her about the grapes, idiot.

'What you're seeing here are the Viognier grapes. We've just passed the flowering stage. Some people start pruning now to let more light onto the grapes but I don't tend to deleaf at this point because the grapes are in full sun here all afternoon. If they get sunburnt, it'll make the skins weaker; if we get heavy rain afterwards, they'll become swollen and split and rot sets in so they'll be useless for making wine.'

'They look like tiny peas,' she said, lifting some of the leaves to look at the grapes and taking a shot.

Her hands were beautiful. Delicate. And he could still remember what they felt like against his skin. How shy she'd been, the first time she'd touched him. How her confidence had grown over the weeks until she matched him heat for heat, passion for passion.

He swallowed hard. 'They'll grow hugely now,' Xavier said. The grapes. Not his body. Though that was reacting, too, and he was glad that he hadn't tucked his shirt into his jeans. It would spare both their blushes.

'Which means we have to keep on top of the weeding,' she said, clearly remembering something she'd read. 'But we're organic, so we don't spray, right?'

'No herbicides or systemic pesticides. We use cover cropping instead.' He indicated the area between the rows of vines. 'Sure, the grass and clover might look a bit scruffy, but it means the soil doesn't erode as much, nitrogen goes back into the soil and we get much more biodiversity. It's a great habitat for insects, which eat the pests.'

'But under the vines it's clear,' she noted.

'We hoe them by hand, to make sure there are no weeds choking the vines.'

By hand.

Allegra could imagine Xavier hoeing, focused on his work. Maybe he'd take his shirt off in the heat, and the sunlight would gild his skin.

She swallowed hard. Clearly the sun was addling her brain, despite her hat. And she really needed a drink of water. Except the film in her head kept unfolding. Memories. Xav, in the middle of a hot summer afternoon, tipping his head back to drink from a bottle of water. His throat working. Closing his eyes, pouring the rest of the water over his head to cool him down. Droplets of water glistening on his bare chest.

Oh, hell. She really had to get a grip. He shouldn't still be able to affect her like this. Though she had to admit he'd grown even better-looking with age. He was still self-assured, but he'd lost the cockiness and arrogance of youth.

'When it's August, it will be *veraison*,' Xavier continued.

'When the grapes change colour.'

He gave her an approving look, '*Exactamente*. Since you've obviously been reading up, do you know how I test them?'

'You taste them?'

The words were out before she could stop them.

Taste.

Just as he'd tasted her yesterday.

Just as she wanted him to taste her, right here and now, under the hot Mediterranean sun.

'I like to check the numbers as well,' he said. 'August is the month when we rest, gearing up for the harvest in September—when things go crazy.'

'You work every single day? And you're in the fields every day?' she asked.

'Mostly, yes—and, no, before you ask, I don't expect you to do the same. It's my land. Part of me.'

He had the sense of belonging that she needed so very much. And how she envied that.

'Though if you're still here in two months' time—'

He really didn't think she would be?

'—you'll be roped into harvest, because we need all the help we can get. We hand-pick because it's better—it does less damage to the clusters and we can select the best bunches. Even Guy joins us in the fields. We'll be working from dawn until late and the days just blur into each other.'

He made it sound like torture, but his expression showed how much he relished it.

'I'll look forward to it,' she said coolly. 'My first proper harvest. I was always back at school when harvest started.' Except that last year, when her parents had been in London in the September before she'd started university, and Harry had encouraged her to leave early and spend some time with them. Build a few bridges.

That last year, when leaving France had been so hard. She'd seriously thought about giving up her place at university and staying with Xav.

And then, when he'd pushed her away, she'd been hugely relieved that she hadn't done anything so rash.

She lifted her camera, doing her best to act as if she were completely casual about this, and began taking photographs. Ostensibly of the vineyard, although somehow Xavier ended up in the frame of a few of them.

'You have a good zoom on that?' he asked.

'Yes, why?'

'Move very slowly, and look to your left.'

She did so, and saw a gorgeous copper-and-black butterfly on one of the leaves. 'It's beautiful,' she whispered, taking the snap. 'What is it?'

'A *papillon petit nacré.*'

'In English?'

He shrugged. 'No idea. You'll have to look it up. But, if you like butterflies, go and take a look in the lavender.'

'It might make a nice picture for the blog. Thank you.'

He drove her down the road to see the Grenache and the Syrah.

'What about the other wine I tasted?' she asked. 'Or was that pure Syrah?'

He blinked. 'Clos Quatre, you mean? That's Marselan.'

'Marselan?' She didn't recognise the name.

'It's a relatively new grape,' he explained. 'A cross between Grenache and Cabernet Sauvignon.'

'I liked it,' she said. 'Do we sell much of it?'

'No. It's my private stock.'

She frowned. 'How do you mean, private stock?'

'It's not part of the vineyard,' he explained. 'Our customers love our rosé and the AOC, but we've made it for years and I wanted to try something a little different. Marselan's grown more in the Languedoc region than here, and it's not a particularly heavy cropper, so it wasn't fair to make Harry bankroll half of my experiment.'

'So you buy the grapes from Languedoc?'

'No. I bought a small clos down the road, about four years back.'

A fourth clos—hence the name of the wine.

And she noticed that he didn't offer to show it to her. That hurt, though she knew she was being ridiculous: it was Xav's personal venture, nothing to do with Les Trois Closes, so there was no reason why he should take her there.

Instead, he took her to the production plant and explained the process of making the wine, from the

grapes arriving from the field through to bottling the
final blend. Allegra took copious notes as well as photographs: maybe she could do a 'day in the life of a grape'
type piece.

'Enough for today, I think,' Xavier said.

'Yes.' Her head was spinning and it'd take a while to
absorb all this.

'Any questions before you go?'

This was the perfect opportunity. 'Actually, yes. You
know you offered to lend me a car, the other day—did
you mean it?'

He looked surprised. 'Why do you want to borrow a
car?'

'Because...' She took a deep breath. Given that her
dog would spend a fair amount of time on his land, this
was something she probably ought to float by him. 'I
wanted to go to the animal rescue centre. There's this
dog...'

He frowned. 'Dog?'

'Harry always had a dog. And I...' She stopped. Telling
him that she was lonely, when she'd only been here a
few days, was tantamount to showing weakness.

'You seriously want to get a rescue dog?'

She nodded.

'They'll want to know that the dog is going to a good
home. That you know about dogs, how to care for them,
and the dog won't be left on its own all day.'

'I thought he could come with me to the office,' she
said. 'And, um, I was hoping you might be able to vouch
for me, if I need a character reference.'

He blew out a breath. 'A rescue dog needs a lot of
attention, Allie. We're gearing up for harvest, the busiest
time on the domaine. It's going to be noisy, with lots of
people about and machinery going. Is it fair to bring a

dog who's maybe had a bad time into that kind of environment, when nobody has time to spend with him and settle him in properly?' He spread his hands. 'And what if you decide this isn't what you want to do, and you go back to London? What then? Does the dog have to go back to the rescue centre and hope that someone else will take him, or are you going to put him in quarantine kennels for months?'

'I'm staying, so that isn't an issue,' she said, lifting her chin.

'You haven't thought this through.' He shook his head. 'Wait until harvest is over. If you're still here and you still want a dog, then I'll help you. I'll drive you to the rescue centre myself and vouch for your suitability.'

He'd been fair. More than fair. And she knew he was right: this wasn't the right time for a dog to settle in. But disappointment lodged in her throat. 'Thank you. I'll see you tomorrow,' she muttered.

'Tomorrow's Saturday. I don't expect to see you until Monday.'

'You'll be working, though.'

He shrugged. 'Just absorb your notes. Maybe do some more tasting—Harry has a good cellar. See if you can tell the differences between vintages.'

'Sure. Um, have a nice weekend.' Feeling that somehow she'd lost some of the ground she'd gained, she packed her things in her laptop bag, secured it in the basket on the front of her bicycle and went home.

CHAPTER SIX

On Saturday morning, Allegra began sorting through Harry's office. He'd always filed everything away neatly, so it wasn't an onerous task—though she had a lump in her throat when she discovered that he'd kept all the letters she'd sent him over the years.

There were photographs, too. A big box full of them, in no particular order. Summers blurred together: when she was eight, fourteen, eleven. Eighteen, all dressed up for a night out in a group with Xav, Guy and Guy's then girlfriend, Hélène. Older pictures, too: a man just recognisable as her father, in his late teens. A younger boy—maybe also her father? And other people she didn't even begin to recognise.

And there, at the bottom, was a photograph in a folder, which was clearly by a professional photographer rather than a family snap. She caught her breath as she opened it and saw the bride and groom smiling into each other's eyes. The groom was Harry, though the bride was a total stranger. Allegra had never seen a photograph of the woman before, and she'd certainly never heard her father talk about any aunt in connection with Harry.

So who was Harry's bride? And what had happened to her?

She went to make herself a cup of coffee and found Hortense in the kitchen, making what looked like ratatouille. '*Bonjour*, Madame Bouvier.'

'*Bonj*—' Hortense began, looking over at her, then stopped with a frown. 'Are you all right, Allegra?'

'Yes and no.' She wrinkled her nose. 'I've just found this photograph of Harry on his wedding day. I had no idea Harry had ever been married—and nobody's ever mentioned his wife.'

'It was a long time ago. I was a child myself,' Hortense said, surprising her. 'They honeymooned here when my mother was the housekeeper.'

'Was she French?' Was that why Harry had left England years ago and settled in France—to please his bride?

'No, she was English.'

'What happened?' Allegra asked, not at all sure she wanted to hear the answer.

Hortense grimaced. 'It was very sad. She died in childbirth.'

'Oh, no.' Allegra clapped a hand to her mouth. She'd thought maybe they'd got divorced—though, given that Harry looked in his twenties in the photograph, the wedding must have taken place in the 1950s, which meant that any divorce would've been seriously messy, not to mention difficult to arrange. But this…this was even more unexpected. And shocking. Poor Harry. 'Did she die here?' Allegra asked. 'And, if so, shouldn't Harry be buried next to her, instead of in a grave on his own?'

'She was buried in London. He came here after it happened.' Hortense lifted a shoulder. 'They'd been happy here.'

Allegra bit her lip. 'I wish I'd known. I mean, I lived in London—I could've put flowers on her grave for him and made sure it was kept clean.'

'He had an arrangement with a florist near the cemetery.' Hortense spread her hands. 'You will need to cancel that.'

Allegra shook her head. 'Absolutely not. I'll keep it going—it's what Harry would've wanted. And I'll make sure I put flowers on his grave, on the same day as flowers go on hers.'

Hortense looked approving. 'He would like that.'

'I really had no idea. I don't even know her name,' Allegra said.

Hortense blew out a breath. 'It was the same as yours, *ma chère.*'

Allegra stared at her, barely able to believe it. 'I was named after her?'

'You'll have to ask your parents.'

Which was easier said than done. Charles and Emma Beauchamp were touring somewhere in Russia, as far as Allegra knew. She could send them an email, but that didn't guarantee a quick answer, especially for something that didn't concern their work. A phone call was completely out of the question; when her parents weren't performing or sleeping, they were practising, and Allegra had learned at an early age never to interrupt their work. She still remembered the day she'd wandered into their practice room and touched one of her mother's violins. The mark of her mother's fingers had been imprinted on her skin for most of that day.

Here was the only place she'd ever really felt accepted as one of the family. And having her around must've been a constant reminder of what Harry had lost. His wife, his child.

'You can't change the past,' Hortense said gently, as if her thoughts were written all over her face.

'No.' Allegra blew out a breath. 'I just wish I'd known.'

She spent the rest of the afternoon sorting methodically through the office, but even after she'd eaten Hortense's excellent ratatouille and an omelette, that evening, she couldn't settle.

This was when she really could've done with a dog to hug. Someone who wouldn't judge her, who'd just be company and accept her for who she was. She knew she could ring Gina and talk to her about it—but then, she also knew what her best friend's response would be. 'Get the next plane home and I'll meet you at the airport.'

It would be, oh, so easy.

And it would be running away. Which wasn't what she wanted. She needed to prove to herself that she could make a go of this.

Why hadn't her parents ever said anything about Harry's wife? Well, that was an obvious one. If it wasn't connected to music, it didn't even register with them. But why hadn't *Harry* ever confided in her?

That hurt.

A lot.

Completely out of sorts, Allegra decided to go for a walk. Exercise was meant to be good for lifting your mood, wasn't it? Given that there was no chocolate in the house and Nicole's shop would be shut, endorphins were about the best she could do. And she might catch some of the sunset, if she was lucky; it might take her mind off things and stop her brooding.

Almost unconsciously, she found herself heading for the small lake that straddled the boundary between her land and Xavier's. It had been her favourite thinking-place in her teens. Though it had also been the place where she and Xavier had made love for the very first time, in the dusk of a summer evening. She remembered every second of it. The way he'd made her feel. Her shyness as he'd begun to undress her, the worry that she wouldn't quite live up to the glamorous girls he'd dated before, and then all the fears dissolving as she'd seen the wonder in his eyes, the tenderness as he'd touched her.

How she'd loved him.

Ten years ago. So much had changed in those ten years.

She sat down by the shore of the lake, wrapping her arms round her legs and resting her chin on her knees, and watched the dragonflies hovering above the water on gauzy wings. The sight was enough to lift her mood and stop the blues settling in too deeply.

Then she became aware of a movement beside her and looked up.

Xavier.

He was the last person she wanted to see right now; but, given that the lake was on the border of their land and she was actually sitting on his side, she couldn't exactly tell him to go away. She was the one who was trespassing.

'Watching *les libellules*?' he asked, gesturing to the darting dragonflies.

She nodded.

'Are you all right?'

'Fine,' she fibbed. Then she sighed. 'Not really.'

He sat down next to her, drawing his knees up and linking his hands in front of his ankles, the way she had. 'What's the matter?'

She opened her mouth, about to tell him that it didn't matter, but the words spilled out regardless. 'I've been sorting through Harry's things. I found this photograph of Harry on his wedding day. His wife shared my name.'

Xavier looked surprised. 'And you didn't know?'

'Not a thing.' She bit her lip. 'Poor Harry. He must've been lonely. If only I'd *known*.'

'Would it have made a difference?'

'Yes,' she said fiercely. 'It would. Because I would've come back earlier. I understand now why he didn't mind me coming here for the summers—I suppose I was as near as he'd get to a grandchild. And maybe there's some family likeness. Obviously not of Allegra herself but of…' She choked. 'I can't believe how bloody selfish my parents were. My father must have known about it. He must've known that Harry had lost his wife and baby in one fell swoop, and yet…' She shook her head, anger curling her lip. 'He just dumped me with Harry for the whole of the summer without giving a damn about how either of us felt about it.'

'Not necessarily,' Xavier said softly. 'Harry must've been in his mid-twenties when it happened. Was your father even born then?'

Allegra thought about it. 'He was a toddler, I suppose—but even so, he must have known the family history. Surely my grandparents told him. And why didn't any of them ever tell me?' She stared at him. 'How come you know about it?'

Xavier shrugged. 'Papa was fifteen when Harry first came here. He once told me that when Harry arrived, he was the Englishman with the sad eyes. Papa overheard his parents talking one day about how Harry had spent his honeymoon here, and his wife and baby died in London the following year. He came back here because he had only happy memories of the place.'

'To be a widower so young, to lose the love of your life and your child in such a way—that's terrible.' Unshed tears stung her eyes. 'And I had no idea.'

'He loved you,' Xavier said drily, 'so he didn't want you to be upset. That's probably why he made the effort to keep it from you.'

She glared at him. 'If I'd known, things would've been different. They *would*, Xav. I would never have been so stubborn. I wouldn't have fallen out with him. I would've come back.' She dragged in a breath. 'I know everyone around here thinks I'm a gold-digger who only came back for my inheritance, but this was never about the money. I don't need the money or the farmhouse. This was about...'

Coming home.

She couldn't bear to say the words.

'I know.' He shifted closer to her and slid his arm round her, drawing her against his side. This time, there was nothing sexual about the contact. It felt as though his strength were wrapped round her, giving her courage. Yet she couldn't speak, couldn't thank him—her throat felt as if it were filled with sand. And she wasn't going to bawl her eyes out in front of him. She wasn't going to let him see just how weak and needy she was.

The misery in Allegra's face told Xavier that she was genuinely angry and upset with herself that she hadn't done more for her great-uncle.

'It's not your fault,' he said softly. 'Your family's as dysfunctional as mine.'

'Yours?' She gave him a scornful look. 'Your parents were always there for you when you were growing up—and Guy adores you. He always has. How's that dysfunctional?'

'*Laisse tomber.* Forget about it,' he said. She didn't need to know about the mess of his parents' marriage, the lies and the deceit. But he didn't pull away from her. It was obvious that Allegra was upset, trying to put a brave face on it, and really needed someone to comfort her. And, right at that moment, he was the only one who could do that. There wasn't anyone else. Harry was dead, her parents were away somewhere on tour—and, even if they'd been here, they would've put their music first—and her friends were on the other side of La Manche, in England.

He couldn't just leave her to stew.

Though sitting there with his arm round her made the last ten years melt away. He remembered another evening when she'd been all wide-eyed and trying to keep the tears back as she'd stared at the lake. The end of June. When she'd been anxious about the A level exams she'd just sat, worrying if her grades would be good enough for university. When she'd worried that maybe university would be a mistake, that she'd face the same pressure there that she'd faced at school to follow in her parents' footsteps. That evening, he'd given her a cuddle, to comfort her—and the moment he'd touched her he'd stopped seeing her as the girl next door. He'd seen her as a woman. *Ma petite rose Anglaise,* he'd called her.

He turned his head slightly to look at her, and it was like a replay of that moment. She was looking straight back at him, her whole expression unsure. He could feel the tension in her body.

'We've been here before,' he said softly. Ten years ago, he'd leaned forward and kissed her. And the way she'd responded had blown his self-control to smithereens. Comfort had turned to passion, and they'd both been carried away.

'Don't blame yourself. I was there too,' she said, accurately reading the guilt on his face. 'I wanted it as much as you.'

'It was your first time.'

She nodded. 'And you made it good for me.'

He smiled wryly. 'You don't have to flatter me, Allie.'

'I'm not.' She returned the smile. 'I must have driven you crazy when I was a kid—an annoying little brat who followed you about and cramped your style with all your girlfriends and made a nuisance of herself.'

'That night,' he said, 'I didn't see you as an annoying little brat. I saw you as a woman.' And he'd fallen deeply in love with her over that summer. His arm was still round her now, but for the life of him he couldn't move away. 'You still have those amazing eyes. Deep and dark as the lake at Issarles.' Later that summer, he'd taken her to see the lake in the old volcanic crater, with water the deepest shade of blue he'd ever seen, and they'd made love among the wild flowers. Even now the memory stayed with him. Even now, the scent of wild flowers brought it all back. The softness of her skin against his. Her warmth. And how he'd felt as if he were a different person when he was with her—as if he could conquer the world.

'Your eyes are amazing, too. You always used to make me think of a pirate king.' She gave him a small smile. 'You still do. Especially with that haircut.' She reached up and placed her hand against his cheek, her fingertips moving lightly against the burgeoning stubble on his cheeks.

'Careful, Allie,' he warned.

When she didn't move her hand away, he turned his face and pressed his lips to her palm. Unable to help himself, he curled his free hand around hers. How soft her skin was, unlike his own work-roughened palms. He kissed the pad of each fingertip in turn, then drew a tiny path of kisses down over the heel of her hand to her wrist. He could feel her pulse beating hard against his mouth, and his senses were filled with the light floral scent she wore.

Oh, hell. This had happened yesterday and it had all gone wrong. Badly so.

He had to stop this right now.

But, for the life of him, he couldn't. It seemed the most natural thing in the world to lean over Allegra, drawing her gently down onto the soft grass. Just as he had all those years ago. Now, as then, her eyes were wide and trusting. Her pupils were huge, telling him that this was affecting her exactly the same way that it affected him. That she wanted him just as much as he wanted her.

His hands were on either side of her body, and he was careful not to squash her with his weight—but right now he really, really needed to kiss her. Properly. Even though his head was saying that they shouldn't be doing this, that he'd told her he wouldn't kiss her again, and here he was doing exactly that. Breaking his word. How dishonourable could he get?

But then her hands slid under the hem of his untucked shirt and splayed against his back, feeling the play of his muscles. Skin to skin. And Xavier lost it completely.

He bent his head and touched his mouth to Allegra's. Her lips parted, opening under his, and he deepened the kiss, sliding his tongue against hers. Her mouth was warm and sweet, and her hands were drawing him closer, her fingertips pressing against his back. She tasted of summer and it made his head swim.

How long had it been since he'd last wanted someone this much?

He couldn't remember and didn't care. All he could think of was Allegra and the fact that she was kissing him back.

When he finally broke the kiss, he traced the outline of her jaw with his mouth. She tipped her head back, offering him her throat, and he responded with hot, open-mouthed kisses all the way down her throat, swirling his tongue against her skin.

She gave a tiny whimper of need—the smallest, smallest sound, but it was enough to shock him to his senses.

Feeling guilty, frustrated and out of sorts, he pulled himself away from her and shifted to a sitting position.

'Sorry. That shouldn't have happened. It was…'

Mad. Crazy. Irresistible, and he wanted to do it all over again, except this time take it to its proper conclusion. With her naked and in his bed.

'We were supposed to have a truce.'

'Uh-huh.'

'It wasn't meant to involve kissing.' And he didn't dare look at her, because he knew he'd just yank her into his arms and kiss her again. 'You and me, it's complicated,' he said ruefully.

'There's a lot of unfinished business,' she said. 'We need to talk. Properly.'

'But not tonight. You're upset and I'm tired. If we're going to do this, really sort it out between us so we can move on and have a decent professional relationship, we need to be on an even keel before we tackle it.'

'You're right.' She sighed. 'Why can't things be simple?'

They were, in one sense. He wanted her, and the way she'd responded to him told him that she wanted him.

But as soon as he started thinking, things started to get complicated. A mixture of resentment and anger and guilt and yearning and... The emotions made his head spin.

'Come on. I'll walk you home,' he said.

'There's no need. I'll be perfectly safe.'

He knew that. He could see the farmhouse from here. But he'd still feel better if he saw her home. 'Humour me?'

She clearly saw it as the request it was, rather than an order, and nodded.

Though he didn't help her to her feet. And he made absolutely sure there was distance between them, enough so that his hand couldn't accidentally brush against hers and then end up with his fingers twined with hers. Because if he touched her now, just once, his control would snap completely.

'Would you like to come in for a coffee?' she asked politely as they reached her front door.

'Tonight, I think that would just make things more complicated.' Because it wouldn't stop at coffee. He could see it in her eyes. She needed comfort—comfort he could give her physically, but then all the past would get in the way and make it even harder for them to move on. 'We'll talk on Monday. And maybe things will be easier.'

'Monday,' she repeated softly.

'*À bientôt*,' he said—and left, before he gave in to the temptation to hold her close and kiss her until the shadows in her eyes vanished.

CHAPTER SEVEN

ALLEGRA slept badly that night; her single bed felt way too big and, even though the night was hot, she felt as if cold radiated all the way through her.

You and me, it's complicated.

He could say that again.

But at least he'd agreed to talk things through with her.

On Sunday, Gina emailed her three different logos and half a dozen different label designs. Smiling, she emailed back, *Thanks, you're a genius and these are brilliant.* Obviously she'd need to discuss it with her co-vigneron and take his views into account, but the one she liked most was the simplest. Three stylised vine leaves, the stems making a knot, with 'Les Trois Closes' in a simple script next to it. With any luck, Xavier would think the same.

And with any luck, things would start to get simpler between them.

On Monday morning, Allegra cycled to the *boulangerie* and the farm shop to pick up her lunch—including a punnet of irresistibly juicy cherries that Nicole told her came from one of the farms outside the village, and a box of *galettes* for the office, which she hoped would give her a friendly start with Xavier's allegedly formidable secretary. She settled herself at Xavier's desk with her laptop and had just started roughing out a list of possible PR activity when she became aware of a shadow by the front door.

She looked up to see a middle-aged woman with steel-grey hair walk in. Thérèse? But she didn't look formidable or bossy, as Allegra had expected; rather than being severely elegant, she was slightly plump with unruly hair and a kind, maternal smile.

'*Bonjour*,' Allegra said with a smile. 'I take it you're Thérèse?'

'Yes, and you must be Allegra. *Bonjour.*'

'I was just about to make some coffee. Can I get you some?' Allegra asked.

'*Merci*, that would be nice.'

When she'd made the coffee, she took the *galettes* through to Thérèse's office as well; half an hour later, they were firm friends. Allegra had made it clear that she didn't expect Thérèse to look after her as well as Xavier, and had cooed over the pictures Thérèse carried around of her five-year-old granddaughter, Amélie, and her brand-new grandson, Jean-Claude. In return, Thérèse had reassured Allegra that having someone to challenge the way he did things would be good for Xavier.

Xavier arrived in the office at his usual time, just before midday. He greeted Allegra with an English, 'Good morning,' but Thérèse was treated to three loud kisses on her cheek and exclamations in rapid French that Allegra couldn't quite follow but, from the smile on his face, it was clear that he was pleased to see his secretary again.

Which was a good thing—but the conversation they needed to have really had to be in private. Clearly it wasn't going to happen in the office. She saved the file on her laptop and shifted to the chair in the corner, letting Xavier have his desk back. He clearly had a lot of admin to do, because he barely acknowledged her for the next hour. He didn't even stop to eat his lunch, instead taking mouthfuls of a sandwich between phone calls.

So much for having a chance to talk to him about the logo and labels and being able to make some decisions. And so much for setting things straight between them.

The next time he put down the receiver, she seized her chance. 'Xavier, there are some things I need to discuss with you about the vineyard. I can see you're busy right now, so would you be free for dinner tonight?'

'Tonight.' His expression turned wary. 'Yes. We need to discuss things.'

'Work things, too,' she said softly.

'OK. Do you want to eat here?'

'I think somewhere neutral might be easier,' she said. 'Somewhere quiet where we can have a decent-sized table in a corner so we can spread papers over it.'

'And discuss things.' He nodded. 'I'll book a table. Though there are some things I need to do in the vines late this afternoon. I'll pick you up at half past six.'

'No need. I'll meet you at the restaurant. Just give me the address.'

'And you'll know how to get there?'

'I can look it up on the Internet.'

He rolled his eyes. 'Don't be difficult. Your bicycle will fit in the back of my car so, better still, we'll go from here and I'll drop you home afterwards.' He glanced at his watch. 'I need to be elsewhere. I'll be back at five, which will give me enough time to have a shower and change.'

She gestured to her jeans. 'And I don't need to change?'

He spread his hands. 'You're not going to be in the fields getting messy. So, no. The place I have in mind doesn't have a strict dress code. See you later.' He said goodbye to Thérèse, then headed out of the door.

Thérèse left at four to go and pick up her grand-daughter from school. Xavier turned up at quarter past five. 'Sorry I'm late. And I'm filthy from the fields. I'll shower and change, and then we'll go.'

'Come and get me when you're done,' she said, striving for offhand.

He raised an eyebrow. 'You've been in the office since before Thérèse arrived and you didn't have a lunch break.'

'Neither did you,' she pointed out.

'We're going to work through dinner, so would it not be better to pace yourself?'

When it was put like that, she could see the sense of it.

She waited while he locked the office, then walked over to the chateau with him. 'Guy will be in his lab; there's no chance he'll come out and be sociable,' Xavier said. 'But if you want a drink, there's coffee, juice and chilled water in the kitchen, through there.' He gestured to the door at the end of the hallway. 'The library's nice at this time of year. There's a good view over Guy's roses if you want to go and sit in there and relax while you're waiting for me.'

'Thanks. I will.'

'I'll be as quick as I can.'

Allegra didn't know the inside of the chateau par-ticularly well; as children, they'd usually been shooed outside by the housekeeper, and when she'd been older Xavier had always picked her up from Harry's. But she duly went into the kitchen. It was a huge room with a terracotta tiled floor, a range cooker nesting in an enormous inglenook and a large scrubbed wooden table in the middle of the room. The cabinets lining the walls were painted cream, and it looked very much as if they were handmade. Next to the inglenook there were open shelves with a rack above it from which hung copper pans; cast-iron cookware sat on the shelves. Another rack contained plates; next door to that was a glass-fronted cabinet containing glassware, and next to the enormous fridge was a tall wrought-iron wine rack filled with bottles.

The worktops were as clear as Xavier kept his desk. She could try to find a coffee maker, but it felt like snooping; instead, she took a tumbler from one of the glass-fronted cupboards and filled it with water from the tap. And she tried not to think of Xavier upstairs, naked and in the shower.

She wandered back into the hall. The first door led to a formal dining room; next was a sitting room; and another opposite that. Again, she was struck by how tidy everything was; every single piece of woodwork was beautifully polished. Clearly Xavier had a housekeeper, because just keeping up with the housework in the chateau would take a full week's work—no way would he have time to do this himself as well as putting in the hours at the vineyard.

At last she found the library. The shelves were filled with an eclectic mixture of volumes in several different languages; there were comfortable sofas either side of an open fire; and the French doors did indeed overlook Guy's rose garden, as Xavier had told her.

On the mantelpiece there were photographs in silver frames: Xavier and Guy at their graduation ceremonies, and a picture of them both with Jean-Paul. But none, Allegra noticed, of Chantal. Which seemed very strange; she knew that family was important to Xavier. Something had obviously happened—though it was none of her business, and she had a feeling that Xavier would be sensitive about it. Given that they already had a tough discussion ahead of them, it would be better not to complicate matters by asking.

But then the baby grand piano in the centre of the room caught her attention. Her upright piano was still in London, and Harry had got rid of his a couple of years ago, according to Hortense.

The lure was irresistible. And hadn't Xavier told her to relax?

She set her glass down on one of the low tables and sat down at the piano. Experimentally, she played a couple of scales. The instrument sounded slightly sharp and needed tuning, but it didn't bother her; this was better than not being able to play anything at all. She began with Lizst's 'Liebestraum', stumbling a little at first and then relaxing into the music. How she'd missed this. Closing her eyes, she let the music flow into her head and played entirely from memory. Chopin's 'Raindrop' prelude, then Satie's 'Gymnopédie number one', finally segueing into Debussy's 'Clair de lune'.

Xavier walked down the stairs, his blood turning to ice as he heard the music coming from the library. Debussy. It took him straight back to his childhood. How he'd loved listening to his mother playing the piano—especially this piece, if he was sitting by the window in the library and watching the rain trickling down the window.

Now the notes sounded like the soundtrack to betrayal, and it rattled him hugely.

He strode into the library, half expecting to see Chantal sitting there instead of Allegra. 'What are you doing?'

To his relief, Allegra stopped playing. 'You told me to relax.'

'Not this way.' The words burst out before he could stop them.

She frowned. 'What's wrong, Xavier?'

Everything. 'The piano's out of tune.'

'A bit, yes, but it's not that bad.'

But maybe some of his tension showed on his face, because then she stopped arguing, slid off the seat and stepped away from the piano.

'I should've got rid of it years ago. Guy and I don't play.'

'Xav, this room needs a piano. And this one's gorgeous. It's so right, here.'

It had been. Once. When the world had been a different place.

'I'm sorry, Xav,' she said quietly. 'I didn't mean to be intrusive. Harry got rid of his piano a while back, and—well, I miss playing.'

He hadn't known that Allegra played the piano, let alone so skilfully. She'd been so adamant that she didn't want to follow in her parents' footsteps, he'd been pretty sure that she didn't play an instrument at all.

And now she looked worried, her lower lip caught between even white teeth.

It was hardly surprising, given his hissy fit. He blew out a breath. 'Sorry. I overreacted.'

'And I intruded. So we're both at fault.' She gave him a rueful smile. 'We're not going to talk about things tonight, are we? On Saturday, I was upset and you were tired. Today, you're upset and I'm tired. You're right, it's not a good combination—not if we want to sort it out without having a huge fight.'

'Maybe we should forget dinner and I should just take you home.'

'We both still have to eat,' she pointed out. 'I don't know about you, but I'm not in the mood for cooking. And there really are some business things I wanted to discuss with you. If today's anything to go by, you're in the fields for most of the day and constantly on the phone when you're in the office. The only way we're going to discuss things is if it's in the evening.'

'A vineyard isn't like an office. You can't work nine to five.'

'I didn't say it was a problem.' She reached out towards him, as if she were going to take his hand—and then stopped, as if she'd thought better of it. 'Do you think Guy would like to join us for dinner?'

'You can try getting him out of his lab, but I don't fancy your chances.'

They paused by the door to Guy's lab; Allegra rapped on it, and Guy appeared a minute or so later, looking dishevelled and resembling a mad scientist. Which, Xavier thought with a rush of affection, was exactly what his little brother was.

'Yes?' Guy asked, frowning.

'I was wondering if you'd like to come to dinner with us,' Allegra said.

'Thanks for the offer, *chérie*, but no. I'm sorting out something here.' Guy made shooing motions with his hands. 'Go and enjoy yourselves, children.'

'It's work,' Allegra said swiftly, as if to make absolutely sure that Guy didn't get the wrong idea.

'So you'll be talking shop all night? Absolutely not, then. I get enough of that from Xav as it is—and he drives me crazy, sampling wines and comparing them to the ones he produces.' Guy smiled at her to take the sting from his words. 'Some other time, perhaps, when you're not talking shop and I'm not up to my eyeballs. *Au revoir, petite.*' He blew her a kiss and closed the door again.

Allegra followed Xavier out to his car. 'Don't you dare say, "I told you so",' she warned.

'As if I would.' He opened the passenger door for her, made sure that she was settled, then hefted her bicycle into the back of his car. When he switched on the ignition, 'Waterloo Sunset' blared through the car; he grimaced and switched it off. 'Sorry. Bad habit,' he said. Given that she'd been raised on classical music—and she'd been playing it herself on the piano, rather than an arrangement of a pop song—she'd probably hate what he was playing. Particularly as it was so loud.

'The Kinks, right?' she asked, surprising him. 'Good choice. So it's just the piano you hate.'

The pieces that made him remember things he'd rather forget. To stop her asking questions, he shifted the focus back onto her. 'I didn't realise you played so well. Didn't you ever consider doing a duet with your mother?'

She grimaced. 'You must be joking! I play for fun, and she plays for perfection.'

He remembered. 'What about your father?'

She scoffed. 'He wouldn't be interested unless I practised twenty-four-seven and was note-perfect on all four Rachmaninov piano concerti.'

'Or the Rhapsody, so you could do a double-bill with your mother.'

She rolled her eyes. 'Oh, please. I can see her standing next to me and smacking me over the head with her violin bow if I dared to play a wrong note. And then my father would insist that I worked on something like Alkan's Grand Etude because it's so fast and so difficult to play smoothly…' She grimaced. 'No, I'd never be good enough for him. And working on something until I met with his approval would take all the pleasure out of it for me.'

'Do they know you play the piano?'

'Absolutely not. I swore my friends to secrecy at school, and Harry would never have dropped me in it—given that he was the one who actually taught me.' She wrinkled her nose. 'I just enjoy playing for me. Sad stuff when I feel blue, happy stuff when the world's full of sunshine. And, actually, I most like playing the Beatles' music. "Eleanor Rigby", "Yesterday"—pieces with a good melody.'

He'd had no idea that their musical tastes meshed so well. They'd never really listened to music, all those summers ago. As children, they'd been too busy playing elaborate games, and when he was old enough to drive, his beloved ancient sports car hadn't actually had a sound system that worked. Jean-Paul had insisted that both Xavier and Guy learned the value of money by paying their own car repair bills, and there was always something on the Alfa that needed fixing rather more urgently than the radio.

'Do you mind if we change the subject?' she asked. 'We're supposed to be discussing the vineyard, not me.'

'Sure. What did you want to run past me?'

'Logos and labels. My best friend works at the agency where I worked—she's a really talented designer. I gave her a brief last week and she's come up with some samples.'

'You gave her a brief. Without talking to me first.' He gave her a speaking look. 'So I get no say in the branding of my own vineyard.'

'You were busy, and I wanted to…' Her voice faltered.

'You wanted to prove yourself,' he finished for her. 'OK. You're the one with the qualifications in marketing.'

'Xav, I wasn't trying to cut you out. I was trying to show you that I can bring something to the vineyard— something different.'

She was trying. And he'd already given her a hard time today, over something that wasn't her fault. 'All right. When we get there, you can show me what she's come up with.'

The bistro he'd chosen was a quiet one. The food was good, the service was unobtrusive, and the chef was an old friend. Once they were settled in a quiet corner, with a glass of wine for her and a bottle of still water for him, and they'd ordered their food, he looked straight at her. 'Right. Talk me through these labels and logos.'

She'd brought a briefcase with her; she took a folder from it and spread four pages across the table. 'These were the ones Gina came up with. I have my favourite, but I'm not going to say which. But I'd like your opinion.'

He picked out the simplest one, the stylised vine leaves. 'I like this one. Three leaves—it fits in with our name, and the colours are for red, rosé and white wine.

Though, strictly speaking, the red I produce is nothing to do with Les Trois Closes.' He studied the piece of paper. 'It's clean. Definitely a case of less is more.'

She looked pleased. 'That's the one I like—for exactly the reasons you just said. Good. We're *d'accord*, then. This is going to be our new logo.'

'*D'accord,*' he said solemnly, disguising his amusement at the way she'd started sprinkling her conversation with French phrases. She really was trying to fit in.

She put the papers away and replaced them with the sample labels.

Xavier shook his head. 'We have plain type on the back of the label now. It does the job. Why replace it with this spiky handwriting?'

'Because the land here is spiky and uncompromising—we're on the edge of the gorges of Ardèche. And the labels will be hand drawn because our wine is made the traditional way, mainly by hand. So then our label reflects the *terroir* and the process—you're an artisan.'

He raised an eyebrow. 'You're calling me a peasant, now?'

'When you live in an ancient chateau? Hardly—I'm calling you a skilled craftsman.'

He smiled, amused. 'You're making a mental note to check your dictionary when you get home, aren't you?'

'I guess I deserve to be teased.'

'No. You're doing OK,' he said.

The delight in her face was quickly dampened down, as if she didn't want him to know that she was pleased by his grudging compliment.

'All right. We'll use the logo. I'm not sure about the labels, though. What's the point of trying to fix something that already works?'

'You have them printed every year, so it doesn't matter whether you use your old typography or the new,' she said. 'If you're trying to broaden your markets, you need to change the labels to reflect customer expectations outside France—which is what these labels do. Speaking as a consumer, I've tried wines simply because I liked the look of the label. If I liked the taste of the wine, it made me try others from the same producer.'

She wasn't going to give up easily. And what she was saying did make sense. Time to compromise, Xavier decided. 'All right. We'll give it a go.'

'Thank you. I also want to set us up on the social networks.'

'They aren't as big in France as they are in England and America,' he warned.

'Fair enough, but if you're trying to widen your markets in England and the States, you need to use the right communications to reach them,' she countered. 'That means viral marketing and word of mouth. Starting with the blog—and, by the way, our hits are rising nicely there—and maybe the odd podcast.'

'Podcast?' Xavier blew out a breath. 'I think I'm beginning to regret agreeing to this.'

He was saved from an argument by the arrival of their food.

'You're right. The food is fabulous,' she said after the first mouthful.

During the meal, she told him of her ideas for promoting their wine, including talking to the local tourist board about a wine-tasting trail, setting up a wine walk round the edges of the vineyard—'So people get to enjoy the wildlife in the vineyard and then taste what we produce at the end,' she explained—and a series of articles in different magazines, each focusing on a different aspect of the vineyard.

But what really impressed him was that she'd included budgets, and ways of measuring the success of the campaigns so they could decide what to do more of in future and what to drop.

By the end of the evening, Xavier was surprised by how much he'd enjoyed talking business with Allegra and seeing her hit her stride. Her enthusiasm was infectious. And she'd grown into a woman he actually liked. A lot.

It would be oh so easy to let himself fall back into a relationship with her. The way she'd kissed him earlier told him that she, too, still felt that zinging physical attraction.

But the past could still get in the way. Mess things up again. He didn't want to risk that.

'It was my idea to go out for dinner, so it's my bill,' Allegra said as the waiter came over.

'You're assuming that I'm a modern Frenchman. Wrong. My bill,' he corrected.

'You can't have it both ways, Xav. You can't see me as the money-grabber who's only come back to France to strip her share of the assets from the vineyard, and then refuse to let me pay for dinner.'

In answer, he simply raised an eyebrow.

'Equal partners, remember,' she said. 'And we have a truce. No fighting.'

He gave her a wry smile. 'All right. We'll split it.'

When they'd paid, Xavier drove them back to their own village. He parked outside Harry's farmhouse—

after years of habit, he still couldn't quite think of it in any other way—and opened the passenger door for her, before taking her bicycle from the back of the car.

'You've given me a lot to think about,' he said.

'In a good or a bad sense?'

'Mostly good,' he said. 'Except the podcast. I'm really not convinced about that.'

'If you want people to start talking about you, you need to do something different,' she said. 'And I think doing a sounds quiz—asking people to guess what they hear—would get us a lot of traffic. People might just come for the fun of the quiz, but if we make the pages sticky enough then they'll see the other, more serious side of the vineyard.'

'Sticky?'

'Give them some interesting things to hold their attention. Interactive and dynamic. The longer they stay on our website and the more they enjoy the experience, the better their opinion of us will be. And it might lead to more orders.' She smiled. 'Let me mock up a few things—and then I'll try it out on you.'

'It's going to be easier to give in than to argue, isn't it?' Xavier asked wryly. 'All right. Our rosé's meant to be about summer and chilling out and having fun. Mock it up and I'll have a look at it.'

'You won't regret it, Xav.' She paused. 'You seem more relaxed, now.'

He had been, but the tension snapped back into him. 'And?'

She took a deep breath. 'The longer we put off this conversation, the harder it's going to be.'

'It's not exactly going to be easy now,' he warned.

'It's probably as good as it's going to get.' She took the door key from her handbag. 'I'll put my bike away. Do you want to make the coffee?'

Hot, strong coffee was probably what both of them needed right now. He took the key. 'Sure. Ready when you are.'

CHAPTER EIGHT

WHEN Allegra came back from the barn, Xavier had made coffee and was sitting at the kitchen table, his hands wrapped round his mug. His face was etched with strain, and her heart ached for him. Even though he'd hurt her so badly in the past, she hated seeing him look so upset now. Part of her wanted to wrap her arms round him and hold him close, tell him everything would be fine—just as he'd held her when she'd been upset by the lake.

But she knew that sex would just get in the way. They'd go to bed, comfort each other—and they wouldn't talk, so the problem would still be there. He was right to have set her mug on the opposite side of the table, rather than next to his. They needed space between them to do this properly.

'Have you ever had an infected scratch from the vines?' she asked.

'Yes, a couple of times.' He looked surprised. 'Why?'

'This is the same sort of thing. Dealing with it's going to hurt, but the bad stuff has to come out before you can heal.'

He took a swig of coffee. 'I'm sorry I had that hissy fit on you earlier. I suppose it caught me on the raw, and I wasn't expecting it.'

'What's so bad about playing the piano?'

He took a deep breath. 'Chantal used to play it. It's kind of... I don't know. Bringing back happy memories, but at the same time they feel tainted.'

'I notice you don't call her "Maman" any more. I take it you fell out with her?'

'Big time.' He sighed. 'You might as well know. She had an affair and left Papa.'

'No way.' It was the last thing she'd expected him to say. She couldn't take it in. Chantal had always been reserved and a bit haughty, but Jean-Paul had been such a sweetheart, so easy to get on with. She could remember him sitting on the terrace outside with Harry, laughing uproariously over some joke or other, and envying Xav and Guy for having a father who was so approachable and interested in his children, unlike her own. 'I'm sorry. It must've been a shock.'

'It was. I always thought with marriage you took the rough with the smooth, and most of the time it *was* smooth. She and Papa were happy—they never had huge fights or bickered, and Papa idolised her. He would've done anything for her.'

'Your father was lovely,' she said, meaning it. 'Why on earth would she...?' She stopped herself, wincing. 'Sorry. That was intrusive. You don't have to answer.'

'Why did she have the affair?' Xavier dragged in a breath. 'She said he wasn't paying her enough attention.'

No wonder he'd made that comment during their fight, about women wanting all your attention. Slowly, she was beginning to understand him a little more.

'I'm still not sure which shocked me most—the fact that she left, or the timing.'

'Timing?'

'We'd had two bad harvests—I didn't know it at the time, because Papa kept it from me, too, but he was putting in crazy hours, trying to keep the vineyard afloat, and the bank threatened to pull our credit.'

'That's awful, Xav.' And no wonder he'd been wary about the website, not wanting to talk about the heritage. He'd said to her that the vineyard hadn't always been successful. She'd had no idea that he'd meant in the recent past, rather than the distant past.

Then a seriously nasty thought struck her. *The timing*, he'd said. 'When did this happen?'

'It doesn't matter.'

'I think it might.'

He was silent for so long that she didn't think he was going to answer. But then he looked straight at her. 'Ten years ago.'

The sick feeling in her stomach intensified. 'After I'd gone to London?'

'The day after Guy's eighteenth birthday,' he confirmed. 'I suppose in some respects we should be grateful that she didn't ruin that for him, too, but the fact that she could plan a party, knowing that she was going to leave the next day...' He shook his head. 'I couldn't stomach the deceit, Allie.'

Guy's birthday was in September, just before harvest. Allegra had been invited to the party but hadn't been able to make it, because she'd been finding student digs—plus her parents had been in London and it had been a rare chance to see them, which Harry had encouraged her to take.

So it had all happened just as Xavier had been due to start his job in Paris.

She needed to know the truth. 'When I called you and asked you to come to London, spend some time with me...' When she'd believed he was in Paris. 'You weren't actually in Paris, were you?'

'No,' he admitted. 'I couldn't leave Papa in such a mess. Losing Chantal devastated him, Allie. She broke his heart. I made him talk to me, and then he told me about the finances—the reason why he hadn't been paying her enough attention. He'd been working crazy hours, trying to keep the business going. The way I saw it, he needed my support—Guy was in his Baccalaureate year, and there was no way either of us would let him throw it all in.'

'So you gave up your job in Paris instead.'

He gave a half-shrug. 'I always knew I'd be coming back here to take over the vineyard when Papa wanted to retire. It just meant that I'd do it a bit earlier, that was all.'

She bit her lip. 'Did Harry know?'

'Yes. He went into partnership with Papa a few months later. He didn't tell you?'

She shook her head. 'I told him that you and I had split up. He told me I was pushing you too hard, we were too young to settle down anyway and I should give you some space.'

'And that's when you fell out with him?'

She nodded.

'Over me.'

'Xav, if I'd only known what was going on... But it felt as if everyone was pushing me about. Harry was telling me what to do, and you as good as told me I was just a holiday romance and you were too busy to see me. I thought you'd met someone else.'

'You weren't a holiday romance. And I *was* too busy to come to London. I was working with Papa to stop the vineyard going under. It wasn't just about us, Allie—it was all the people who relied on us for jobs. We couldn't let them down.'

'Why didn't you tell me what was happening here, Xav?' Regret and anger merged—regret that she hadn't had the chance to support him, and anger that he'd shut her out so completely, hadn't trusted her enough to tell her what was happening.

He blew out a breath. 'Because I was ashamed, I suppose. I didn't want you to know that my mother had run off with someone else after nearly twenty-five years of marriage. And I didn't want you knowing that we were in financial difficulties.'

'I would've understood, Xav.' She swallowed hard. 'If you'd told me—OK, I couldn't have done anything practical to help, but I could at least have been there for you. I could've listened. And if you'd told me you needed me, I would've come back. I would've been there to hold your hand.' She dragged in a breath. 'Your life had just been turned upside down and, instead of being there to support you, I dumped you. You must have hated me.'

'I did,' he admitted. 'I thought you'd let me down as much as Chantal had let my father down. All I needed was some time to get my head together, but you went on and on and on, wanting to know when I was coming to see you. I know I probably snapped at you, but I didn't mean it like that.' He paused. 'You really thought I was seeing someone else?'

'No—well, yes.' She raked a hand through her hair. 'I couldn't think of any other reason why you'd suddenly go so cold on me, why you'd push me away and tell me you were too busy to see me. Xav, I was eighteen years old. I still had a lot of growing up to do. And I was tired of being pushed around, never in charge of my own life. I thought you didn't want me. I had some pride left—so I wanted to be the one who called a halt, not the one who was dumped.'

'So you hated me, too.'

'For a while.' She bit her lip. 'I never wanted it to end between us.' Tears pricked her eyes. 'Xav, that summer, I thought all my dreams had come true. I thought we'd…' She dragged in a shaky breath. No. That was a confession too far.

'We'd what?' he asked, his voice husky with emotion.

'It doesn't matter.'

'I think it does,' he said, echoing her earlier words to him. 'Tell me.'

'Once I'd graduated, I thought we'd…' She blew out a breath. 'I thought we'd get married.'

'Me, too. I was going to ask you to marry me that Christmas,' he said. 'In Paris. I was going to sell the car so I could get you a really spectacular ring. And I was going to take you to the top of the Eiffel Tower and ask you to marry me.'

She could see the truth of it in his face. That, back then, he'd loved her just as much as she'd loved him. And he'd been willing to sacrifice his beloved car to get her a flashy ring, because he'd thought that was what she'd wanted? 'You know, a silver ring off a market stall would've been enough for me,' she said. 'I didn't need anything flash. I didn't *want* anything flash. I only wanted you.' He was all she'd ever wanted.

His breath hissed. 'How did we get it so wrong?'

'I misinterpreted the way you were acting. I had a lot of growing up to do. But I wouldn't have hurt you, Xav. Not for the world.'

'And I never meant to push you away, make you feel that I didn't want you.' He sighed. 'I guess I needed to grow up a bit, too.'

'If only we'd talked—really talked—back then. But you can't change the past. There's no point in endless recriminating.' She so, so wanted to reach out to him. Just holding his hand would be enough. But she could still see the wariness in his face; so she held back, keeping her fingers wrapped firmly round her mug. 'Do you see your mother at all?'

'Not much,' he admitted. 'I found it pretty hard to forgive her. Papa loved her so much. Losing her meant he'd lost a part of himself. But he loved her enough to let her go, give her a divorce so she could marry this guy.'

'She married him?'

Xavier shook his head. 'It didn't last. Neither did the next three—I sometimes wonder whether she measured them up to Papa and realised she'd made the biggest mistake of her life.'

'Would your father have had her back?'

'Like a shot. He was still in love with her right until the day he died. But she just stayed away. I wish he'd found someone else, someone who would've made him happy and loved him back the way he deserved. But he only wanted Chantal.' He gave her a wry smile. 'That's the thing about Lefèvre men. They have a habit of falling in love with the wrong woman.'

That stung. And it wasn't true. 'You and I weren't wrong, all those years ago.'

'Maybe. Maybe not. We weren't strong enough to last.'

There was nothing she could say to that. Ten years of being apart said that he was right.

'Papa threw himself into work. I put in the same hours, but it just didn't occur to me that he was so much older than I was—that he needed to slow down. Not until he had his heart attack.'

He blamed himself for his father's illness? 'Xav, it wasn't your fault.'

'That's what he said. So did Guy. But it felt like it,' he admitted. 'I did call Chantal, when Papa was in hospital. I asked her if she'd come and see him.'

'Did she?'

'She said she'd think about it.' He looked away. 'I don't know whether she would've come or not, because he died before she made up her mind.'

'Xav, that's so sad.' And she could understand now why he'd shut off. He'd lost everything except the vineyard and Guy: and that kept him going now.

'I haven't seen much of her since. Guy found it easier to forgive her—I guess because Papa and I didn't tell him about the business problems at the time. We thought he didn't need that kind of pressure when he had exams on the horizon.' Xavier shrugged. 'Guy trained in Grasse, which isn't so far from Cannes, and he saw her again there. It took him a year to admit it to me. I think he thought I might disown him over it.' He gave a rueful smile. 'We had a bit of a fight. But he made me see another point of view. She was a middle-aged woman who panicked when she realised that she was heading for forty, thought my father wasn't paying attention to her because she was old and unattractive—she had no idea that he was trying to save her from worrying about the business—and she made a really stupid mistake.'

'Maybe if your father had shared his worries with her, she would've understood.' Just as Allegra herself would've understood, had Xavier confided his worries in her instead of pushing her away.

'Maybe,' he said. 'We'll never know, and, as you said, we can't change the past.'

'So where do we go from here?' she asked.

'I don't know. Trust is a bit of an issue for me,' he admitted. 'What with my mother lying to Papa and running off, you dumping me and then Guy's wife deciding that he wasn't paying her enough attention while he was building up the perfume house…'

'Guy's divorced?'

'Yes. And Véra took him for every Euro she could.' He gave her a cynical smile. 'You could say, like father, like sons. There's a bit of me that thinks the men in my family just aren't any good at finding "the one".'

'Or maybe they're just too proud,' Allegra said. 'Maybe they need to open up, let their partners close and realise that it isn't weak to share your worries.'

He shrugged. 'Who knows?'

'And you still don't trust me.' She shook her head in exasperation. 'It doesn't help that I only came back here after Harry died.'

'You told me why you didn't make the funeral. I understand that. It wasn't your fault,' he said.

'Actually, it was my fault. I should've been stronger and stood up to my boss. I should've refused to go to

New York and told him that my family was more important, and that people who put their job before their families don't make good employees because they can't empathise with others.' She bit her lip. 'But I wanted that job. So badly.'

'Do you still want it?'

'That's academic—he appointed someone else.'

'Let me rephrase it. If you had a second chance of having that job and keeping it, would you still want it?'

She considered it. 'No. I loved working at the agency, but I wouldn't go back now, even if I was offered the job that should've been mine and a huge payrise.'

'So what do you want?'

Xavier. It had always been Xavier. But was he too damaged to give them another chance? 'I don't know,' she prevaricated. 'Maybe we should take this day by day. Maybe we can become friends.'

'There's a problem with that. I can barely keep my hands off you. My office in the middle of the afternoon, the lake, the other evening... Even now, there's a bit of me that wants to kiss you until we're both dizzy. I want to carry you up to bed, right here, right now.' He blew out a breath. 'And that's not fair to either of us. I'm not looking for a relationship, Allie. I just want to concentrate on building up the vineyard and make wine that people really love.'

'So you're saying that it's going to be business only between us?'

'Business only,' he confirmed. 'It's the best thing for both of us.'

She wasn't so sure. But it was the best he was going to offer her. 'You trust me to work with you, then?'

'Now we've had this conversation…yes. I think we both know where the other's coming from, now. We've got a shot at making this work. As a business.' He stood up, and took his still-full mug over to the sink. He poured the coffee down the drain and rinsed out the mug. 'For what it's worth, I'm sorry I hurt you all those years ago.'

'I'm sorry I hurt you, too.'

'I'll see you in the office. Goodnight, Allie.' And he walked out of the door.

CHAPTER NINE

BUSINESS only, he'd said. And, over the next few days, Allegra seemed to go into overdrive. Every day she had something to show him: a proof for the new wine labels; new word-processing templates for the vineyard's letterhead and compliments slip, bearing the new logo; and more entries in her 'Diary of a Rookie Vigneronne'.

She might not be doing any of the physical stuff, Xavier thought, but she worked just as hard as he did. And she was clearly intent on proving just how much she could bring to the vineyard.

'I've got quite a few magazines interested in features on us,' she informed him on the following Monday. 'There are three definites: one on life as an English expatriate in France; one on the change from a hectic City lifestyle to a rural environment; and one on the biodiversity in our vineyard. We should get quite a bit of interest from those.'

'That's good.' And something he hadn't thought of doing, even if he'd had the time.

'Obviously I need to take photographs to go with the features, so is there anything you'd rather I avoided? I mean, of course I'll ask the team for their permission before I take pictures of them working or what have you, but I'd love to be able to offer a series—something like a year in the life of a vineyard,' she said.

Given that magazines had long lead-times, she was clearly planning much further ahead than their two-month trial. And although Xavier knew that her show of commitment should've made him relax, it only made him feel warier. It was like building a house of cards. The more she put into it, the more it would collapse.

'I'd better take you round to meet everyone properly,' he said.

She positively beamed at him. 'Great. When?'

'Tomorrow morning?'

'Fine. Do you need me here at the crack of dawn?'

If he said yes, he knew she'd do it. But he wasn't going to push her that far. 'Whenever suits you. Just call my mobile when you're ready to leave, and I'll pick you up.'

She shook her head. 'I can't drag you away from work. Tell me where to go, and I'll meet you there.'

'It'll take me ten minutes, tops,' he said. 'But if it makes you feel better, I'll meet you here at the office.'

'OK. I'll call you when I'm here.'

And so he found himself outside the office at half past seven the following morning. Allegra was wearing jeans, sensible shoes, a loose cotton shirt and a broad-brimmed hat trimmed with a chiffon scarf the same shade of cerise as her shirt, the same way she'd dressed years before. Xavier was really glad that he was driving, because it meant that he had to concentrate—and his hands had something to do other than remove her hat and draw her close to him so he could bend his head to kiss her.

Oh, for pity's sake. He was working crazy hours to keep her out of his head. It had to start working soon—surely?

He introduced her to the team working on the field, and the way they responded to her unsettled him further. Even the most taciturn of them talked to her about what they were doing; her questions were sensible and showed her true interest in what they were doing, so they became expansive, showing her how to do things and encouraging her attempts and giving her enough time to make notes. And when she told them about the articles and her blog—in French, he noticed—not one of them refused to have their photograph taken. She'd clearly managed to charm them all.

By lunchtime, she'd made friends with all of them and knew their families and histories—and they treated her as if she'd always been part of the vineyard.

'That was brilliant,' she said as he drove her back to the office. 'They've got great ideas about the kind of wildlife I should be recording and the best time to see them, and what kinds of sounds would be interesting for the podcast.'

'They're a good team.' Xavier had known them for years and trusted them implicitly; but he'd never thought of asking the estate workers for their views on promotion. He'd concentrated on the vines and the produce.

'Xav, I know I'm going to be more of a hindrance than a help at this stage, but I'd like to do my bit here. Even if it's only an hour or so a day, or you just give me, say, half a row to look after. I want to be more than just the woman who sits in the office and talks to people. I want to be a real part of the vineyard.'

Put like that, how could he refuse? It was how he felt about the place, too. 'As long as you pace yourself. It's a lot hotter here in the south of France than it is in England,' he warned.

'I can take direction,' she said softly, 'as long as I know the reasons behind it.'

'In other words, you don't want to be bossed around just for the sake of it.' He remembered what she'd said about being pushed around.

'Exactly.' She smiled at him. 'So would you be happy if I, say, do an hour's work in the fields, then walk around a bit with my camera in the mornings?'

'Happy' wasn't quite the way he'd put it. In the fields, he was at least away from her and didn't have to fight the attraction—unlike in the office, when he was intensely aware of every single movement she made and had to rein himself back all the time. But he couldn't think of a decent reason for her not to be there. She was his business partner, and the best way of finding out exactly how a business worked was to do every job yourself or shadow someone else. Her suggestion made complete and utter sense—except where his emotions were concerned. 'Sure,' he lied.

Over the next few days, Allegra did an hour's work in the fields in the morning, then went round the vineyard making notes, taking photographs and recording sounds before going back to the office and putting in a full afternoon's work there. By the end of the week, he knew he was falling under her spell again, no matter how hard he tried to fight it.

Late on Friday afternoon, everyone else had gone home and Xavier was checking on a row of vines that he'd been concerned about when he became aware that someone was walking down the row towards him.

Without looking up, he knew it was her, because the back of his neck was tingling.

What was she doing here? Why wasn't she in the office, or heading for home? He always sent everyone home early on Friday.

'Hi.' She gave him a shy smile.

The midday heat had died down, so there was absolutely no need for him to feel this dopey. 'Hi.' Damn, and his voice *would* have to croak.

'You sound thirsty.'

He was. For her. Though he kept his mouth resolutely shut; he simply nodded and hoped she'd be fobbed off by it.

'Here.' She handed him a water bottle, chilled to perfection.

'Thanks,' he mumbled, and tilted the bottle to his lips. And almost choked when it occurred to him that she'd probably sipped earlier from exactly the same spot.

She patted his back. 'Are you OK, Xav?'

'Yes. Thank you for the water,' he said, when he'd recovered.

'Pleasure.' She met his gaze, then deliberately drank from the same spot.

Was she *flirting* with him? His libido responded instantly, and he immediately hoped she wouldn't notice his arousal.

'Do you have five minutes?'

If his libido had been a dog, it would've been wagging its tail madly, sitting up and begging.

'I wanted to run something by you,' she said.

Then he noticed that she had her laptop bag with her.

Work. He could manage that. 'Sure,' he said.

He let her lead him to a quiet spot by the trees, and sat down beside her. She powered up the laptop, then slid it from her lap to his. 'Let's see how sharp you are,' she said, giving him a truly sassy smile.

Her 'sounds' quiz, he realised. Definitely something different; and he managed to get eight out of the ten sounds.

'Tut, tut, Monsieur Lefèvre. And I expected you to get a perfect score.'

No, he was far from perfect. But, right at that moment, looking at her with the sun shining on her hair and her eyes sparkling, she was. France had softened her. Without her business suit, she was just how he remembered her, that summer, all warm and sweet and adorable. And, despite her floppy hat, she'd caught the sun slightly and there was a dusting of freckles on her nose. This wasn't the cool-headed businesswoman sitting next to him. This was the girl he'd fallen in love with all those years ago.

'What are you thinking?' she asked.

How beautiful you are. Not that he had any intention of telling her that. Or acting on the crazy impulse to kiss her. *'Ce n'est rien,'* he said, resorting to a Gallic shrug. 'So when's it going live?'

'Next week.'

Once they were back to talking about work, the dangerous moment was averted. But Xavier was all too aware of how easy it would be to let things slip back to how they'd been, ten summers ago. Part of him wanted it; but the cynic in him wondered. If they hit a problem with the vineyard, was she right and talking about it with her would help with his worries? Or would she misinterpret him again and walk out? He didn't know, and that was the problem: until he could trust her, and trust his judgement where she was concerned, he had to keep his distance. For both their sakes.

Another week went by, and Allegra thought that Xavier was starting to lose that wary look with her. She'd taken to dropping in to the café/farm shop on the way home and trying one glass of a different wine, and making notes about it in her tasting diary. Nicole was highly amused by it, but made plenty of good suggestions; and Allegra tried to catch Xavier at lunchtimes and talk her discoveries over with him.

Working in the fields boosted her confidence further; she was beginning to feel a real part of the vineyard now, part of the team. Even the day when she got blisters from hoeing was bearable, because Xavier noticed—he smoothed cream on her hands, and there was a tenderness in his touch that disarmed her. He made her sit in the shade for a while and, as if he noticed how frustrated she was at not being able to do what everyone else was doing, he sat with her and talked through the week's schedule, to make her still feel part of it all.

Late on the Wednesday afternoon, they were walking through the vines together while she took photographs for the blog. Usually it was cool enough to be bearable at that time of day, but right then the air was close and heavy.

'It's going to pour in a minute,' Xavier said, looking up at the sky. 'We'd better head back.'

Allegra put her camera back in its pouch and slung it round her neck before following him back through the vines.

They were half a row from the edge of the field when the rain hit—huge, fat drops of water. Xavier took her hand and ran for the belt of trees at the edge of the field, pulling her along with him. The canopy of leaves was enough to protect them from the worst of the rain, but they'd been far enough into the fields to be drenched already. Allegra glanced at Xavier; the rain had plastered his T-shirt to his body like a second skin, exposing the width of his shoulders and the hardness of his muscles, and no doubt she was equally exposed.

Her heart seemed to skip a beat and all her senses were heightened; she could smell the rich earth, feel the sudden coolness in the air now that the oppressive heat was broken, and hear the raindrops drumming on the earth around them.

She glanced at him again to discover that he was looking straight back at her, his gaze trained on her mouth and then lifting up to her eyes again. She had no idea which of them moved first, but then he was cupping her face in his hands. He lowered his head and brushed his mouth against hers once, twice; her lips were tingling, and it wasn't anywhere near enough to be satisfying. She needed more. As if he sensed it, he dipped his head again and nibbled at her lower lip. She opened her mouth to let him deepen the kiss, and his tongue slid against hers, teasing and exploring and demanding and coaxing and inciting, all at the same time.

When she kissed him back, everything seemed to vanish; she was only aware of Xavier, the strength of his body and the warmth of his mouth. His hands had moved to splay against her spine, holding her close to him, and her arms were wrapped tightly round him. She didn't care that they were both wet; she just wanted him to keep kissing her and touching her, until the tightness in her body eased.

And then he broke the kiss.

She almost whimpered with frustration and need. Until she looked at him and saw the same need and frustration in his expression.

The rain had stopped, and steam was rising from the earth.

'We'd better get you out of those wet clothes,' he said.

'Yes,' she whispered, knowing that she was saying yes to a lot more than just dry clothes. She wanted to feel the weight of Xav's body over hers; and she desperately wanted to wrap her legs round him and urge him deeper inside her.

Xavier's fingers were entwined with Allegra's as they walked back to his car. His head was telling him this was utterly crazy and he shouldn't do it, but for the life of him he couldn't stop now. This had been a long, long time coming. Maybe once they'd made love it would break the tension between them and put everything back to normal, he told himself. Maybe it would get this desperate craving out of his system—and hers. The way she'd kissed him just now told him that she needed this as much as he did.

He opened the passenger door for her, then climbed into the driver's side. And he managed to stall the engine when he tried to start the ignition. Worse, he'd left the air conditioning on, so the blast of cool air against his rain-soaked skin made his body tighten further. Then he made the mistake of glancing at her. The cool air had had exactly the same effect on her body, and her nipples were clearly delineated through the wet cotton of her T-shirt. He couldn't stop himself reaching over and tracing the curve of her breast with one fingertip, swirling it round her nipple.

She murmured her consent, and he lost it completely. He dragged her over towards him and dipped his head, opening his mouth over her nipple regardless of her clothes and sucking hard. Her fingers slid through his hair, urging him on, and her body arched against him.

He had just enough strength left to release her. Heaven only knew how he drove them back to the chateau. But, the next thing he knew, they were standing on the cool terracotta floor of his utility room, and he was peeling off her wet clothes. Getting her exactly how he wanted her to be. Naked.

Dieu, she was so lovely. All woman. And he wanted her so badly, it actually hurt.

He stripped off his own clothes, before bundling them into the washing machine.

But when he turned back to Allegra, he discovered that she'd gone shy on him. Her eyes were wide with worry, and her hands were strategically placed to cover herself.

'What's wrong?' he asked, as gently as he could.

'What if someone comes in?'

'They won't.'

'How do you know?'

'Guy isn't here. He's in Cannes. There's just you and me here, right now.'

She bit her lip. 'What about whoever does your house?'

'She works mornings only.' He took a step closer to her. 'Allie, stop panicking and stop talking. *Just kiss me.*'

He lowered his mouth to hers; this time, Allegra was the one to deepen the kiss. His hands came up to cup her breasts, taking their weight, and he teased her nipples with the pads of his thumbs. Pleasure lanced through her, but it still wasn't enough. She wanted more—so much more. She broke the kiss, arched her body against his and tipped her head back, offering him her throat.

He made a murmur of assent and drew a line of kisses down her throat, hot and open-mouthed; her skin tingled at the contact. One of his thighs was nudged between hers; she could feel the heat and strength of his erection pressing against her. Despite the fact they'd both been soaked in the rainstorm and the floor was cool, her skin felt super-heated. Any second now, she was going to implode.

He dipped his head farther, just as he had in the car, and took one nipple into his mouth. Except this time there were no barriers; and the feel of his mouth against her drove her crazy. She pushed her fingers into his hair, urging him on.

To her shock, he stopped. And then he stooped slightly and scooped her up into his arms.

'Xav!' She clutched at his shoulders.

'It's either carrying you to my bed or taking you on the floor right now,' he warned her, his eyes hot with desire. 'While I have a shred of civilisation left in me, I'm going to give you the chance to say no.'

Absolutely not. She wanted this as much as he did. She wouldn't mind betting that right now her eyes were as wild as his and her mouth looked as reddened and ravaged as his did; and it thrilled her that she'd done this to him, that she'd broken his iron control over his emotions and he was letting go for her.

'I'm saying yes,' she said, and then grinned. 'Whoops, forgot my manners. That's a yes, *please.*'

In response, Xavier carried her straight up the stairs; he kissed her all the way there, and she didn't have a clue whereabouts his bedroom actually was in relation to the stairs. All that mattered was that he'd carried her there and laid her gently on his huge double bed, an old-fashioned brass frame with a thick mattress, deep, soft pillows and amazingly soft, smooth bed-linen that smelled of lavender.

The mattress dipped beside her; he kissed her once, very lightly, then took his time exploring his way down her body, kissing and stroking and inciting until she was burning hot for him. Her breathing was shallow and she was actually quivering with need. He slid his hand between her thighs and stroked her skin, getting nearer and nearer to her sex but stopping a whisper away.

She dragged in a breath. 'Xav, I'm going crazy here.'

'With you all the way, *ma belle.*'

'Please,' she begged.

And then at last he drew one fingertip along her sex. She quivered at his light touch, teasing at first and then more focused, swirling with just the right pressure.

Though it still wasn't enough.

'More,' she whispered.

He slid one finger inside her.

'Please.' The word was ragged and didn't even sound as if it came from her. 'I need you inside me, Xav. Now.'

He shifted his weight so he could open the drawer in the cabinet next to his bed and took out a condom. She heard the foil packet ripping; then he rolled it on and shifted so he was between her thighs. She saw his biceps flex as they took the weight of his body—and then finally, finally, he fitted the tip of his penis against her sex and pushed, easing into her.

She could still remember the very first time he'd made love to her, the day he'd taken her virginity by the lake and blown her mind. Then, he'd paused to let her body adjust to the feel of him inside her, and he did exactly the same now. He dipped his head to brush his lips against hers, and whispered, 'OK?'

'Very,' she whispered back. Physically, Xavier was perfect, and he knew exactly how to give her pleasure.

'Hold on, *ma belle*,' he told her, his voice cracked, and began to move. Slowly at first, then harder, faster, sending shocks of pleasure rippling through her body.

She'd forgotten just how good this could be. Sure, she'd had lovers since her relationship with Xavier, but she'd never committed to them, and none of them had been as skilful a lover as Xavier. None of them had ever matched up to the man she'd thought would be her one and only.

She slid her hands round his neck and tangled her fingers in his hair; it was so soft, so silky, beneath her fingertips. Then she drew his head down to hers and kissed him deeply, exploring his mouth with her tongue, mimicking the action of his body inside hers.

The pressure built and built and built, drawing her closer and closer to the peak; she broke the kiss, tipping her head back against the pillow and pushing up hard against him, taking everything he could give and wanting more.

And finally her climax hit, pleasure splintering deep inside her.

She opened her eyes and looked straight into his; she could see the exact moment that he reached the peak, too.

'Xav,' she whispered.

He jammed his mouth over hers, kissing her hard, and she felt his body pulse within hers.

At last, he eased out of her.

She stroked his face, brushed his lower lip with the pad of her thumb and smiled. They didn't need words; what they'd just done transcended all. And now everything was going to be all right. She settled back against the pillows and pulled the sheet over her while Xavier went into his en suite.

But, when he came out, everything seemed different. He'd left the bed relaxed and smiling, but she could see the tension in his shoulders as he walked towards the bed, and his mouth was set.

'What's wrong?' she asked softly.

'I'm sorry.'

She frowned, not understanding. 'What for?'

'I owe you an apology. This shouldn't have happened.'

She stared at him. This couldn't be possible. They'd just made love; and she was pretty sure it had been as good for him as it had for her.

He raked his hand through his hair and sat on the edge of the bed. 'We agreed. We're business partners.'

'It's not as simple as that, and you know it. Xav, just now, you were there with me. All the way. It was completely mutual. We both wanted this—*needed* this.'

'I can't offer you anything other than a business relationship,' he insisted.

She wasn't buying that. 'Only a few minutes ago, I saw you completely lost to pleasure. Inside me,' she emphasised.

Colour slashed across his cheekbones. 'OK, I admit it. I find it hard to keep my hands off you.'

At least he admitted there was a physical connection between them.

But she was pretty sure it went deeper than that. When they'd had that heart-to-heart, he'd told her that he'd planned to ask her to marry him. Their break-up had been a stupid misunderstanding; they'd both been hurt by it, but now they understood each other better. It was time to start healing.

'Xav. I can't keep my hands off you, either. We're good together. So what's the point in fighting it?'

He shook his head. 'This is just physical.'

No, it wasn't. It was more than that for her. She liked the man Xavier had become. Responsible, fair, treating his staff with respect and expecting more from himself than he did from them.

If she was honest about it, she'd never really stopped loving him. She'd hidden it away, not wanting to be hurt any more—but that was the real reason why she'd never wanted to commit to anyone else. Because she loved Xavier. Always had, always would.

And she had a feeling that that was why he hadn't committed to anyone, either.

He was in deep, deep denial.

How was she going to haul him out?

'You want me and I want you,' she said. 'If I kissed you now, you'd kiss me back.'

'And I'd resent you for it,' he said. 'Allie, I told you. I have trust issues.'

'You think I'm going to let you down again?' That hurt. Hadn't he listened to a single thing she'd told him? Hadn't she shown him how it could be? 'Xav, I've worked with you in the vineyard. I've learned a lot from you, and I think I've taught you things, too. We're a good team.'

'I know. Business isn't the problem.'

'Then what is?'

'I can't shake the fear, Allie,' he told her. 'I can't help wondering what will happen if we have another set of bad harvests, like we had when my parents split up, or there's some other problem at the vineyard.'

She couldn't believe what she was hearing. 'So you think I'm going to be like your mother and just bail out?'

'You came back to France to escape your job in London,' he pointed out. 'The day you found out you'd inherited half a vineyard, you resigned.'

She blew out a breath. 'That's unfair.'

'But it's true.'

'Well, yes. But that's different. The problem with my job had been dragging on for months.'

'Business problems can drag on for months.'

'So you're saying we have to keep each other at arm's length because you don't trust me.'

'Or my own judgement. Not where you're concerned. I've got it wrong on so many levels, before now.'

She bit her lip. 'You're not even going to give us a chance, are you?'

'I don't want to hurt you, Allie.'

Too late. He already had.

'What's it going to take to make you trust me?' she asked.

'I don't know.' He raked a hand through his hair. 'God help me. If I knew that, I could fix this. But I don't. I can't.'

She felt her eyes narrow. 'This works two ways, though. Xav, how do I know that you're being open with me—that you haven't still got this weird masculine idea that you need to protect delicate little me from anything difficult, and you're holding out on me?'

'You don't and you can't,' he said simply. 'So now do you get what I'm trying to tell you?'

She hated it…but, yes, she did. And until she could find some way of persuading him to see her point of view—that they could work it out if they took the risk and trusted each other—she'd just have to live with this. 'You have to be the most stubborn, awkward man I've ever met.'

'I'll take that as a compliment.'

'It isn't one, believe me.' She grimaced. 'I would offer to give you some space, but would it be possible for me to borrow some dry clothes, first?'

'My clothes would drown you.' He sighed. 'Look, the washing cycle should've finished by now. I'll go and put your stuff in the dryer.'

'Can I borrow a T-shirt or something in the meantime? Because I'd rather not, um, stay here.' In his bed. Where the sheets were still warm from their bodies joining together.

'Sure.' He looked uncomfortable. 'Um, would you mind looking away?'

'Of course.'

He frowned. 'What's so funny?'

Clearly he'd noticed that she hadn't been able to stop the momentary quirk of her lips. 'We just had sex. Hot sex. Completely *naked* sex. It's a bit late for modesty, Xav.'

'Yeah, you're right.' He brazened it out and strode over to the chest of drawers.

She knew she ought to look away but, heaven help her, she couldn't. Physically, Xavier Lefèvre was the most perfect man she'd ever seen. Utterly beautiful. And she wanted him so badly.

He pulled on his underpants, then went to his wardrobe and dragged out shorts and a T-shirt. 'Help yourself to whatever you want,' he said, gesturing to the wardrobe. 'I'll be downstairs. If you want a shower, there are clean towels in my bathroom.'

Clean towels, and the woody shower gel he used that made her feel as if his arms were still wrapped round her. She washed her hair, wrapped it in a towel, then dried herself and went in search of something to wear. The best she could come up with was one of his white cotton shirts; it would show no more flesh than if she'd been wearing a short dress.

Just as long as she didn't bend over, because there was no way she was borrowing any of Xavier's underwear.

She borrowed his comb to take the tangles out of her hair, then padded downstairs to the kitchen.

Xavier's eyes widened when she walked in, and she could see the surge of desire in his face, quickly damped down.

God, he really was the most stubborn man she'd ever met. Didn't he realise that this thing between them wasn't going to go away? Ten years ago, she'd convinced herself that she didn't care and she was over him, but it wasn't true. And she was pretty sure he wasn't over her, either.

'Coffee?' he asked.

'No—I'm fine, thanks.'

'I would suggest a walk in the garden, but it's raining again.'

She gave him a wry smile. 'Xav, you can talk as much as you like, but it's not going to go away.'

'Yes, it is.'

She walked over to him and rested her hand on top of his. 'Let me do one thing for you.' She could at least make the library and the piano less difficult for him, bring back some of the pleasure he'd once had in it—just as Harry had made music a pleasure again for her.

'What?' he asked, looking wary.

Her heart bled for him. Xavier really couldn't trust anything or anyone, could he? 'Come with me,' she said softly, and led him to the library. 'It's up to you whether you sit next to me or as far away from me as you can—but let me take away the bad memories for you.'

He flinched as she sat down at the piano. 'Just don't play Debussy.'

'I'm not going to.' She started to play 'Waterloo Sunset', stumbled a bit, changed the key, then began humming along. She glanced over at him. 'You're supposed to join in.'

'What?'

'Given how loud the stereo is in your car, you obviously sing along to it. So do it now.'

He looked as if he was fighting himself, but eventually he joined in. And he had a good voice, strong and in key.

'See? It's not so bad. This is how I get rid of the blues, Xav—and it's the best way I know. Now give me another song.'

He blinked. 'You can play absolutely anything by ear?'

'If I know the tune, yes.' She rolled her eyes. 'Don't look at me like that. It's not exactly difficult if you've played for years and know where the notes are.'

'Allie, normal people can't do that.'

'Yes, they can. So don't tell me I've inherited my parents' musical genius. I'm just me. And this is about fun, not relentless pressure.' She started playing a Beatles tune next; looking resigned, he gave in and sang along.

By the time she'd finished playing, he looked a lot happier—though he was still not sitting next to her.

She closed the lid of the piano, walked over to him and laid her palm against his cheek. 'There's good stuff in life, Xav. You just have to look for it and let people in.'

He looked surprised. 'But the way you grew up, practically ignored by your parents and dragged around in their wake...'

'I had Harry,' she said simply. 'And, actually, he was the one who showed me that music could be fun instead of the endless quest for perfection that my parents made it. He used to play like this with me, when I was little. He'd play all the famous songs from musicals. Actually, he could've been a professional musician.' She sobered, and blinked away the threatening tears. 'Ignore me. I'm being ridiculous.'

'No, you're not.' He drew her close, cradling her against his body. 'Allie. I wish it could be different. But something broke in me ten years ago. I'll only hurt you. And I don't want to do that.' He rested his cheek against her hair. 'It's better for both of us.'

'That'd sound more convincing if you didn't have your arms wrapped round me,' she said. And regretted it when he promptly loosened his hold.

'I'll go and check if your things are dry,' he said.

He was being a coward, and they both knew it, but she couldn't bring herself to call him on it. He'd already told her more than she'd expected, and no doubt now he was panicking about how vulnerable opening up to her had made him.

She sat back down at the piano. She was just going to have to take it a bit more slowly. But she'd show him that this could work. That together they could be amazing.

It would just take a bit of time until he believed her.

CHAPTER TEN

OVER the next few days, Xavier steadfastly tried to resist Allegra—but even when he was in the fields, he found himself looking out for her, and he despised himself for being so weak. Hadn't he learned from what had happened to his father? No way was he going to put himself in that situation: loving her so much that he'd fall apart when Allegra eventually got bored with the vineyard and decided to leave.

But, God help him, he couldn't take his eyes off her. He couldn't sleep at night, remembering how her hair had been spread out over his pillow and how he'd felt inside her, as if everything was right with the world.

And then an opportunity arose: a meeting in Nice to discuss options with a new distributor. Which meant he'd be miles away from Allegra, that he'd finally have some space to think.

Though Allegra had other ideas when he told her. 'What do you mean, you're going to Nice to talk with a distributor?'

'It's a good opportunity.'

'Then I'm coming with you.'

'You really don't need to.' Although he made sure he sounded casual, inwardly he was panicking. The romantic Côte d'Azur: Cannes, with its sandy beaches and palm trees, its beautiful stone buildings and the harbour, the flower market and the narrow streets in the picturesque old town. Sharing that with her would be irresistible. How was he possibly going to keep his head? He could see himself walking hand in hand with her in the sunset, the sea swishing gently onto the shore.

No, no, no, no, no.

'It's my vineyard too.' She folded her arms and glared at him. 'I'm going with you.'

'You'll be bored,' he said.

'I need to learn about distribution.'

'The discussions will be entirely in French.'

'Not a problem. My French is nowhere near as rusty as it was a month ago. And if I miss anything you can always fill me in later.'

Every single argument he made, she had a counter-argument for it.

In the end, he was forced to agree.

And then it got worse.

'Nice is off,' he told her as he put the phone down.

She looked up from her laptop. 'So when do we reschedule?'

'Not when. Where.' He took a deep breath. 'Paris.' The City of Light was the most romantic city in the world. The Seine and its *bateaux-mouches* all lit up at night, the cafés in the Latin quarter playing jazz, Montmartre with its street artists and the Sacré-Coeur at the top, the Eiffel Tower lit up like a golden beacon at night over the city and sparkling on the hour.

The place where he'd planned to propose to Allegra at Christmas, ten years ago.

'Paris.' Her face went white.

'You don't have to go.'

'No, it's fine.' She lifted her chin. 'Paris it is.'

So, early on the Tuesday morning, he drove them both to Avignon, where they caught the TGV to Paris. He spent the entire journey forcing himself to concentrate on sets of figures on his laptop, though he was intensely aware of Allegra beside him: the floral scent she wore, and the fact that she was humming softly to herself as she worked on her own laptop.

Although she was wearing one of her sharp business suits, he knew the softness that lay beneath, and it was driving him crazy.

When was he going to stop wanting her?

They had just enough time to check into the hotel before their meeting with Matthieu Charbonnier, the distributor. And Xavier found himself clenching his fists when the older man went straight into charm mode and kissed the back of Allegra's hand—particularly when she blushed and responded.

Oh, for pity's sake. He had no right to be jealous. He was the one who'd called a halt on their affair.

But the feelings just wouldn't go away.

When Matthieu realised that Allegra was English, he insisted on conducting their business in English. And he was delighted with the new bilingual labels that Allegra had produced. 'These will definitely help in the English-speaking market,' he said. 'I like the new look. Clean yet traditional, like your wines.'

'Allie's idea,' Xavier said shortly.

'And a very good one. Now, which competitions have you entered, this year?'

'None.'

'Pity, because your wines are good. Even if you only get a silver or a high commendation, it still carries weight on the English and American side of the market,' Matthieu pointed out. 'If you want to widen your distribution, maybe you should think about it for next year.'

'Are we too late to enter for this year?' Allegra asked.

'Not if you sort it out in the next couple of days,' Matthieu told her.

'We don't need to enter competitions. It's all hype. The wine speaks for itself,' Xavier said, feeling even more out of sorts. He steered the conversation back to the wine and distribution options. Finally, they agreed terms, shook each other's hand, and Matthieu promised to have the draft contract sent to their lawyer.

'And how charming it was to meet you, Allie,' he said, bowing and kissing Allegra's hand again.

'You, too.'

He gave her his business card. 'Just in case there's anything else you want to discuss with me. I would have liked to offer you dinner tonight, but I'm afraid I have to be in London. But some other time, perhaps?'

Over Xavier's dead body. And he shook Matthieu's hand just a little too firmly as the older man said goodbye.

'That went well,' Allegra said brightly. 'I'm glad I came.'

'Mmm.' Xavier wasn't glad. At all. He was as jealous as hell, and it unsettled him even more. Why couldn't he think straight where Allegra was concerned?

She glanced at her watch. 'Do we have any more business to sort out this afternoon?'

'No. Why?'

'It's just…it'd be nice to see a bit of Paris.'

He stared at her. 'Have you never been to Paris?'

'Only to the airport and the train station.' She bit her lip. 'I know you probably have tons to do so, if you don't mind me playing hooky, I'll find a tour or something.'

'I'll show you round.' The words were out before he could stop them.

'Really?' She beamed at him. 'Thanks. I'd appreciate it. It's so much better to visit somewhere with someone who actually knows the place and can tell you about it.'

He could hardly disappoint her by changing his mind now. But maybe if they walked everywhere, he'd wear them both out enough to keep their hands off each other. 'Can you walk in those shoes?' he asked.

'Sure I can.'

'We're not going to have time to visit everything,' he said, 'so either we can go and walk around the Louvre or we can just tour the outsides of some of the more favourite buildings.'

'What are the chances of spending tomorrow here and visiting the Louvre properly then?' Allegra asked.

He knew he should say no. But the appeal in her wide eyes was irresistible. 'OK. We'll start at Notre Dame.'

He took her over to the Île de la Cité and let the beautiful gothic cathedral speak for itself.

'Xav, this is stunning,' she whispered, gesturing to the huge rose windows.

'So are the views from the tower. It's the best place to see the gargoyles.'

'Can we?' she asked.

She was delighted by the strange carvings and, although Xavier had seen them several times before, seeing them with her made him see them anew. And not just the gargoyles; all the beautiful buildings in Paris seemed just that little bit more sparkling, seen through her eyes.

'I think we've earned ice cream,' he said when they reached the bottom of the tower stairs again. Though he didn't have just any old ice cream in mind. He wanted Allegra to experience the best of the city he'd loved so much as a student.

He took her over the bridge to the Île Saint Louis and bought her a *fraise de bois* ice cream.

'This is amazing,' she said, after her first taste. 'I've never had ice cream this good before. Thank you.'

'Pleasure.' He smiled back at her. 'It's the best in Paris.'

She eyed his cornet. 'So what's yours?'

'Caramel.'

'Is it as good as this?'

'Would that be a hint that you want a taste?'

She grinned. 'Yup.'

He offered her the cone but, to his shock, instead of licking the ice cream, she reached up and touched her mouth briefly to his.

'Mmm. That's good.'

Her voice was low and breathy, and sent desire lancing through him. 'My control only goes so far, Allie,' he warned.

Her smile told him that she was perfectly aware of that and had kissed him deliberately.

As they walked along his hand kept brushing against hers and his skin was tingling; he could feel his control starting to splinter.

'We're going to the Eiffel Tower,' he said, and shepherded her to the RER station near the Notre Dame.

He'd planned to walk up all the stairs to the first stage, but he'd noticed that she was starting to flag, so they took the lift instead. Though it really didn't help that he was squashed next to her and she fitted perfectly into the curve of his body. How easy it would be to slide his arms round her and draw her back against him. And even easier to dip his head and kiss the curve between her shoulder and her neck.

Even though the whole of Paris was spread out before them, the only thing he could see was Allegra's skin, all soft and smooth. And he *wanted*.

'The view's amazing,' she said softly. 'So why is Paris called the City of Light?'

'*La Ville-Lumière*? Because of the street lighting at night—it was set up earlier in Paris than in most places,' Xavier explained. 'Plus the lighting now. We have so many beautiful buildings, and they need to be shown off.'

'I'd really love to see Paris lit up at night. Do you think we could maybe have dinner somewhere overlooking the city?'

He couldn't resist the appeal in her eyes. 'Sure.' He glanced at his watch. 'They're about to close, here. Let's go back to the hotel and change.'

A cold shower helped his common sense take over again. Waiting for her in the hotel reception also helped. But then she walked into the reception area, and Xavier was really glad he was sitting down because he'd just gone weak at the knees. Allegra was wearing a sleeveless dress in raspberry-coloured silk georgette, knee length and swishy; there was a rose corsage in the same material on the left of the deep V-neck. She'd teamed it with suede high heels in the same raspberry colour with a rose detail on the toe, her hair was up in a chic twist, and she was wearing a choker of black pearls with a black agate rose in the centre. Her make-up was minimal, but in any case her amazing midnight-blue eyes didn't need any emphasis. She was gorgeous just as she was.

This was his *petite rose Anglaise* all grown up.

And he didn't want to take her out for dinner tonight; he wanted to carry her straight to his bed and loosen her hair before taking her clothes off, very, very slowly.

He kept himself in check—just—and took her to Montmartre.

'This is beautiful,' she said as they wandered through the ancient streets.

'It's where many of the artists lived,' he told her. 'Degas, Matisse, Renoir and Picasso.'

'I can see why it attracted them. Do you know the area well?'

'Given that I was a student in Paris?' He slanted her a look.

She rolled her eyes. 'Of course you do. You know it as well as I know London.'

He smiled. 'This is my favourite part of Paris—even though it's pretty touristy in places. And then there's the Place du Tertre—it's just north of here and during the day it's full of street artists.'

'Would we have enough time to come back tomorrow?' she asked. 'I'd love to see the Sacré-Coeur properly, too.' She gestured up to the pure white basilica.

'Sure.' He led her through the back streets to a tiny bistro, somewhere he'd been before and knew the food was good. 'Would you like some wine?'

'Just one glass,' she said.

Something reckless in him made him order champagne.

'Celebrating something?' she asked.

No. He'd just wanted to drink champagne with her. 'Our new distribution deal,' he said.

'To Les Trois Closes,' she said, lifting her glass.

He echoed the toast and clinked his glass against hers.

'So why don't we enter the wine competitions Matthieu talked about?'

He wrinkled his nose. 'It's a lot of admin. It really isn't worth the fuss, whatever Charbonnier says.'

'If you say so.' She smiled at him. 'Though did you notice that he liked the new labels?'

'You're fishing.'

She laughed and sipped her champagne. 'Humour me.'

'OK. I admit that you were right, Mademoiselle Beauchamp, and I bow to your superiority.'

Then he wished he hadn't been so sarcastic when she gave him the most wicked look. 'I'd rather you knelt.'

Oh, *Dieu*, the pictures *that* put in his head.

When their meal arrived he had no idea what it tasted like; he could only focus on her. And it was even worse when the sky started to darken outside and the waiters lit candles on every table. Why had he been so stupid as to think that he could cope with such a romantic atmosphere?

When they'd finished, the waiter came over to ask what they wanted for pudding.

'Will you trust me to order for us?' he asked Allegra.

'Sure.'

'We'll have *le moelleux*,' he said decisively. 'With two spoons.'

She arched an eyebrow when the waiter had left. 'You're sharing a pudding with me, Xav? Isn't that a bit risky?'

Way too risky. He brazened it out. 'It's *the* Parisian pudding, but no way can you eat a whole one on your own.'

'Is that a challenge?'

He smiled. 'No. I wouldn't dare challenge you.'

'Pity.' She moistened her lower lip with her tongue. 'I enjoy a challenge.'

Oh, *Dieu*, she was flirting with him again. And now he was imagining her doing that to his mouth. Astride him. Without that dress.

When the pudding arrived, she smiled. 'Ah. So it's a chocolate fondant pudding.'

'Not "a",' he corrected. *'The.'*

'I love chocolate puddings.' She looked at him through lowered lashes. 'They're so *sensual.*'

He groaned. 'You're doing this on purpose, aren't you?'

'Moi?' She gave him a teasing smile. 'I have no idea what you mean.'

Then she dropped her spoon. 'Oops.'

'I'll get you another.'

'The poor waiters are rushed off their feet. Let's be kind to them and share a spoon.' She eyed the spoon, and then his mouth. 'It's a long spoon. If I lean forward slightly...'

She did so, and he couldn't help following the line of her dress, seeing how her cleavage deepened. And he remembered touching her skin. Tasting it.

He cracked and fed her a spoonful.

She gave a deep sigh of pleasure. 'That's fabulous.' She took the spoon from him—his skin burned where she touched him—and fed him a mouthful.

It took all his control not to let his hand shake when he took the spoon back.

He managed to survive pudding. Just. 'Coffee?' he suggested, intending to order a double espresso. The caffeine might jolt some common sense back into his head.

'Not for me, thanks.' She stifled a yawn.

'My company's that boring, hmm?'

'No. It's the fresh air and lots of walking.'

'I can take a hint. Let's go back.' He paid the bill swiftly, ignoring her attempts to pay her share, and shepherded her out of the bistro. When she stumbled on a rough piece of pavement, it was only natural that his arm should go round her to support her. And even more natural that her arm should slide round his waist. And then they were strolling through Montmartre like lovers...

He stopped under one of the lamp-posts. 'Allie.'

'Mmm?' She glanced up at him.

He spun her round to face him, dipped his head and brushed his mouth against hers. How sweet she tasted. He'd barely touched his glass of champagne, and yet his head was spinning—all because of her.

'Tell me to stop now, or I can't be responsible,' he said.

'Who says I want you to be responsible?'

'My control's at the point of deserting me,' he warned.

'Good. Because I want you out of control. I want the man I know you are,' she told him fiercely. 'All of you.'

Pure desire skittered down his spine. 'You drive me crazy. I want your hair down and spread across my pillow,' he said hoarsely. 'I want you in my bed and wrapped round me.'

'That's what I want, too,' she said. 'Right now.'

Without another word, arms still wrapped round each other, they walked back to the hotel. By mutual consent, they ended up in his room. The second he closed the door behind them, he unzipped her dress, peeled it off her, and hung it carefully over the back of the chair.

Her smile held a quirk of amusement. He pulled her to him and kissed her with real passion, deep and demanding and hot—and suddenly even the flimsy barrier of her underwear was too much.

Her bra and knickers matched her dress perfectly, he noted: a glorious shade of raspberry, in sharp contrast to the sheer ivory of her skin. He hooked his fingers under the straps of her bra and drew them down to bare her shoulders. *Dieu*, she was lovely. He kissed his way along soft, smooth skin, lingered in the hollows of her collarbones and then traced a path of kisses just beneath her pearl choker.

She gasped and tipped her head back, and he took advantage of the position to loosen the fastenings in her hair and let it tumble to her shoulders. 'Allie, you're amazing, so perfect,' he whispered.

He unsnapped her bra with one hand and let it fall to the floor. When he cupped her breasts and teased her nipples with the pads of his thumbs, she quivered. He was gratified to see her pupils dilate, to the point where her irises were the tiniest rim of midnight-blue.

'Xav, I need to feel your mouth on me,' she said huskily.

He dropped to his knees, and teased one breast and then the other with the tip of his tongue. How amazing the contrast was between the puckered raspberry skin of her nipples and the smooth ivory skin of her breasts; and he just couldn't get enough.

She wriggled, moving closer to him; he took the hint and kissed his way down over her abdomen and along the top of her hold-up stockings. As it was, he seriously considered just ripping the seam of her knickers, but exercised enough control to draw them down, stroking her skin as he did so. He nuzzled her inner thighs and drew his tongue oh so slowly along her sex.

'Xav!'

He felt her knees buckle and supported her before she fell. Then he stood up, scooped one arm under her knees and carried her to the bed. It took him all of three seconds to strip off his own clothing. He grabbed a condom from his wallet; his hands were shaking so much that he had trouble putting it on. Then he knelt between her thighs. 'Now?' he whispered.

'Oh, yes.' Her breath was a hiss of pleasure. 'Love me, Xav.'

He did.

He loved this amazing woman with every fibre of his being. He always had. He'd hated her for a while, when he'd thought she'd let him down—but now he knew they'd had crossed wires. If only he could get past this stupid fear and trust her. Trust himself. Love her the way he wanted to.

'Je t'aime,' she whispered, and he stopped being able to think straight; he was so aware of how much he loved her and wanted her and needed her.

Gently, he eased his body into hers; she felt so perfect round him, hot and so ready for him. He pushed deeper and was rewarded by a murmur of pure pleasure. He loved the fact that she was so abandoned to him right now. He kissed her hard; her hands fisted in his hair and she kissed him back, demanding and taking just as much as he was. He felt her body begin to tighten round him, and it tipped him into his own orgasm.

As he came, he whispered, 'Allie, *je t'aime*,' and held on to her for dear life.

Afterwards, she pressed the tip of her finger against his lips. 'Don't you dare say it. I know you're thinking it, but don't *say* it. At least give me tonight.'

He kissed her fingertip. 'I can't think straight any more.'

'Then sleep with me tonight, Xav. I want to wake in your arms tomorrow.'

He wanted that, too. Wanted it so badly.

'Last time…' She dragged in a breath. 'I don't want it to be like last time. I just want you to hold me.'

'I know, *petite*.' He kissed her, and went to the bathroom to deal with the condom. As he came back to bed she propped herself up on one elbow and he could see fear glittering in her eyes. In his head, he knew that this was going to make everything much more complicated—but they'd deal with it tomorrow. Tonight he was going to act on the urging of his heart, not his head, and sleep with her in his arms.

As he slid beneath the covers and gathered her into his arms he could see the relief in her face. *'Tout va s'arranger,'* he said softly. 'Everything will turn out fine.'

Even though he knew he was lying.

The next morning, Allegra woke with her head pillowed on Xavier's shoulder and his arms wrapped round her.

She could hear by his regular breathing that he wasn't awake yet; not wanting to break the spell, she stayed where she was, enjoying his closeness.

When he finally stirred, she smiled at him. 'Good morning.'

'Good morning.'

She could see the panic in his eyes, and stroked his face. 'Hey. This is Paris. It's a stolen day out of time. No discussions, no judgements. We're going to wander through Paris and enjoy it. Hearts, not heads. That's the rule. OK?'

'OK. But we have to get the TGV home this afternoon,' he corrected, 'so I make that half a day.'

'Better get up and make the most of it, then.' She brushed a kiss against his chest. 'Care to join me in the shower, Monsieur Lefèvre?'

His whole body tensed, and she could feel the war going on between his head and his heart. Luckily for her, his heart seemed to win, because he climbed out of bed, scooped her up and carried her to the shower.

After a breakfast of hot, dark coffee and pain au chocolat, they went to the Louvre, and then wandered hand in hand through the Jardin des Tuileries, enjoying the sculptures and the fountains and watching children play with wooden boats on the boating pond. They saw Monet's huge pictures of lilies in the Musée de l'Orangerie then took the Metro back to Montmartre and caught the funicular railway to the top of the hill.

The beautiful white basilica of the Sacré-Coeur was even more beautiful inside, Allegra thought; then Xavier kept his promise to take her to the Place du Tertre, where they wandered through the square full of tables and brightly coloured umbrellas, drinking in the scent of coffee and hot bread from the cafés lining every inch of the square. Over the sound of people chattering, she could hear jazzy guitar playing.

As he'd told her, there were artists everywhere, sketching.

'Can we?' Allegra asked.

'N—' He stopped himself. 'Sure.'

Ten minutes later, she was in possession of an amazing sketch of them together. And Xavier was definitely looking at her as if he cared, she was sure.

Finally, it was time to catch the TGV back to Avignon. Their half a day out of time was over.

As if Allegra was reading his thoughts, she asked, 'So where do we go from here?'

'I don't know,' Xavier answered honestly. 'What do you want?'

She took a deep breath. 'I want a man who wants the same things as me. A man who respects that I'm independent, that I'm an individual and have my own way of looking at things. A man who respects my mind as much as he wants my body.'

He could do that. He could definitely do that.

'And I want roots. I want a man who wants to be in the same place as me.'

Ice trickled down Xavier's spine. 'Which is where? The vineyard?'

'I love it at Les Trois Closes. But…maybe. Maybe not. I don't know.' She spread her hands. 'Right now I'm at a crossroads. I need to make a decision about where I want to be.'

And he could guess what she really wanted. The way she'd spoken to him before about London, about how safe she felt there—she'd want to go back. Back to the safety of her life in London. And her independence was important to her, too: she'd want the place where she could control her own security.

London.

Which meant there was no place in her life for him.

He couldn't settle in London, even for her. The call for home was too strong.

Allegra sighed inwardly. He'd closed up on her again. But she'd been as open as she could with him. She wanted him to see that she was independent and committed, but she wanted a say in things; she didn't want him to run the whole show and dictate all the terms.

'It's your life. Your decision,' he said. 'You're the only one who could make it.'

This was where he was supposed to add, 'But I want you to stay.'

Or was he acting on his head again, convinced that love never worked out and he didn't want to take the risk?

She could slide her hands round his neck, pull his head down to hers, and she knew he'd respond. Physically, they were perfectly in tune.

But she wanted more than just sex. She wanted his heart.

And somehow she was going to have to find a way through all the barriers he'd thrown straight back up.

CHAPTER ELEVEN

THEY drove back from Avignon in silence; with every kilometre, Allegra knew that Xavier was distancing himself from her. When they reached the farmhouse, he took Allegra's case from the back of his car and opened the passenger door.

'Would you like to come in for coffee?' she asked.

He shook his head. 'Not a good idea. You know what will happen.'

She did.

'And you know my feelings about that.' His expression was bleak. 'We agreed that Paris was a day out of time, and now we're back in the real world. Which means we're business partners. End of. Goodnight, Allegra. See you in the office tomorrow.'

Why did he have to be so stubborn about this? She was utterly sure he felt the same way that she did. The night before, he'd even said he loved her, in his own language.

And yet he wasn't going to give them a chance.

The next morning, Xavier was out in the fields when she arrived at the office. She fished Matthieu Charbonnier's card from her handbag and called his mobile. Ten minutes later, she had the information she needed. Twenty minutes after that, she'd entered Clos Quatre into the wine competition online, organised a courier and was busy sticking labels on the wine.

Strictly speaking, she should've asked Xavier first. It was his wine, not theirs.

But she knew he'd refuse, and she wanted to prove something to him. She wanted him to see just how good his wine was and how far he'd come since the days when he'd taken over from his father. And maybe, faced with the proof that she believed in him, he might just start to believe in her.

Over the next week, Xavier avoided her as much as possible. She knew why; this was his way of avoiding temptation. He'd admitted that he could hardly keep his hands off her, and it was the same for her. And yet he steadfastly refused to give in. To the point where he'd even work in the fields during the hottest part of the day rather than face her.

This really wasn't good for him. The second day he did it, she texted him to tell him that she was too hot to work in the office and she was going home for a swim, and for the next week she planned to work just in the mornings at the vineyard office and would be going home in the afternoons.

His reply was brief and to the point. *Merci.*

And she wanted to push him into a pool of icy water, make him wake up. Did he know how unreasonable he was being right now?

Knowing Xavier, he probably did.

She sighed. How could she break the stalemate between them? She was out of ideas, and this was going nowhere. Apart from driving her slowly insane.

In the middle of Thursday morning, Guy walked into the office and sat on the edge of her desk. 'Allie, *petite*. Lovely to see you.'

'Hi. I wasn't expecting to see you. Are you back for a long weekend?' she asked.

'Yes. Are you doing anything this evening?'

She shrugged. 'Nothing important. Why?'

'Just wondered if you wanted to come over for dinner. Right now it's perfect for eating outside.'

'Was that dinner just with you, or with Xav as well?' she asked.

'Both of you. Is that a problem?'

'No,' she fibbed. She'd bet good money that as soon as Xavier found out that Guy had asked her over, he'd make some excuse not to be there. But in a way that would be useful; maybe she could talk to Guy about the situation. He was the most likely person to know what was going on in his brother's head, and he might have some good ideas about how she could persuade Xav to see reason. 'I'll bring pudding,' she said, adding with a smile, 'I wouldn't dare bring wine.'

'Half past seven, then.' He slid off the edge of her desk and blew her a kiss. '*À bientôt.*'

She cycled home via the village and picked up a tarte tatin and a pot of double cream from Nicole. And when she cycled back over to the chateau that evening, Xavier answered the front door.

His eyes widened. 'What are you doing here?'

'I invited her. Don't be rude to my guest,' Guy said, coming into the hall. 'Welcome, Allie. Come in and have a glass of wine.'

'Thank you, Guy.' She handed him the box and the pot. 'I hope tarte tatin's all right.'

'*Absolument*. It's my favourite.' He smiled. 'Given that, resourceful though you are, I doubt you box things up like this, do I take it that this is one of Nicole's?'

'Yes, and she sends her love.' Allegra looked straight at Xavier.

Colour slashed across his cheekbones. 'I'd better get back to the grill,' he muttered and fled.

'Maybe I should just go home,' Allegra said, feeling awkward.

'No. He's been like a bear with a sore head for days. Ignore him.'

Ha. That was easier said than done.

Guy escorted her out to the terrace, putting the apple tart in the fridge on his way, and poured her a glass of rosé. 'I've been reading your Rookie Vigneronne blog. It's great stuff,' he said.

'Thank you.'

'And I like the new labels. Actually, I have to admit I invited you over tonight with an ulterior motive. Would your designer be able to do something for me?'

'I can ask her. It depends how mad things are back at the agency and how big the job is.'

'I'm developing a new perfume and I need a look for it. Maybe you could come to Grasse and I could show you around the perfumery and talk over the brief with you. And maybe if you have some spare time I could ask you to do some work for me, too.'

Being away from Xavier might help. Didn't they say that absence made the heart grow fonder? Or maybe it would be a case of out of sight, out of mind. She glanced over at him—brooding over the grill, and using it as an excuse to avoid her. 'Sure.'

'Thank you, Allie.'

Xavier eventually joined them with a platter of barbecued meats and bowls of salad, and Guy kept the conversation going whenever Xavier and Allegra fell into an awkward silence.

'Xav tells me you've been hiding your light under a bushel,' Guy said when he brought a jug of coffee and three cups through to the terrace.

'Me?' Allegra felt her eyes widen. What had Xavier said?

'I didn't realise you played the piano.' He smiled at her. 'Any chance you'll indulge me and play for us this evening?'

She glanced automatically at Xavier. Just for a moment, before he made his face carefully blank, she was sure she saw longing there—the same longing that filled her whole heart.

'Of course I will,' she said, rather more brightly than she felt.

Guy undid the French doors to the library; she sat down at the piano. Xavier was sitting as far away as he could, she noticed; but she didn't need him to look at her. She needed him to listen.

She played a couple of upbeat, lively numbers.

And then—looking straight at Xavier so he'd know she was playing this for him—she began playing 'Time after Time'. She sang along with it, straight from the heart, silently begging him to listen and understand what she was telling him. That he could let himself trust her because she'd be there. She'd find him if he was lost. Catch him if he fell. She'd be there every single time.

Except he clearly didn't listen—or didn't want to know—because he walked out in the middle of the first chorus.

She stared at his retreating form in dismay, knowing that she'd lost, and stopped mid-song.

Guy came over and gave her a hug. 'Sorry. My big brother's a total idiot.'

Right at that moment, she didn't trust herself to speak; she just nodded and willed the tears to stay back. She'd cried herself empty over Xavier ten years before, and no way was she going to do that again.

Dully, she closed the lid of the piano. 'Thanks for this evening, Guy. I'm sorry I spoiled it.'

'You didn't spoil it, *petite*.'

He was just being kind, and she knew it. 'I'll be on my way home.'

He sighed. 'I'll drive you.'

She shook her head. 'You can't. You've been drinking.'

'Only one glass, so I'm well under the limit, *chérie*. I wouldn't take stupid risks.'

'But I came on my bike.'

'With my car, that would be a teensy problem—but there's an easy solution. I'll use Xav's.' He shepherded her into the kitchen and grabbed Xavier's keys from a drawer.

He hefted her bicycle into the back of the car, opened the passenger door to let her in, then climbed in the other side and switched on the ignition. 'You really love him, don't you?'

'I never stopped.' Her voice cracked. 'How obvious do I have to be, Guy? I'd give him everything I am. But he's never going to let himself trust me. And my being here isn't good for either of us.' She dragged in a breath. 'So I'm going back to London.'

Guy's eyes widened. 'You're bailing out on him?'

'I can't make him love me, Guy. And I'm only making him unhappy, being here. He can do what he likes with the vineyard—I'm not going to sell it, but I'm not going to get in Xav's way.'

'Ah, *chérie*, I wish things could be different.'

'So do I.' But they weren't. And it was about time she faced it instead of fooling herself and opening herself to further hurt.

Guy drove her home, settled her at the kitchen table and made her a mug of hot chocolate. 'Are you sure you're going to be OK?'

'Yes.' She kissed him on the cheek. 'Thanks, Guy. For looking after me. For caring.'

'Of course I care. You've been my friend since we were little.' He gave her a hug. 'If you need a friend, you know where I am.' He took his wallet from his pocket and pulled out a business card. 'Do you have a pen?'

She found one in her handbag; he scribbled a number on the back of the card. 'This is my personal mobile, as opposed to my work mobile. Call me any time.'

'Thanks, Guy.'

If only it had been Xavier making that offer.

But she knew now it was never going to happen.

Twenty minutes later, Xavier looked up as Guy pulled the plug of his computer from the wall in his office. 'Hey! I was working on that.'

'Tough.'

'I hadn't saved my file.'

'Tough,' Guy repeated, folding his arms. 'For some-one usually so astute, you're being really dense. You do realise Allie's in love with you?'

'And?' Xavier drawled.

'Oh, for pity's sake. Don't start spouting that rubbish about Lefèvre men not being able to find the right one. Papa and Maman—they had a lot of good years before it went wrong. And don't bring my marriage into it, either. Véra and I should never have even got engaged because we just weren't compatible. It was my fault as much as hers.' Guy shook his head in frustration. 'Do us all a favour, Xav, and think about it. It's been ten years, and Allie never got married to anyone else. Neither did you. That's because you're meant to be together.'

Xavier rolled his eyes. 'You've clearly been in your lab too long and the chemicals have muddled your thinking.'

'Face it, *mon frère*, you're in love with her and she's in love with you, and right now you're running scared. Stop being such an idiot. It's the chance to get your life back on track, the way it should be, with a woman who's going to give you everything she is and expect everything you are in return. You're lucky you've found the right one.'

'I can't trust my judgement where she's concerned.'

'Then trust mine.' Guy shrugged. 'It's up to you. If you want to be an idiot, I can't stop you. But I'm telling you, if you have a grain of sense left in you, you'll ring Allie now and apologise, tell her you're as mixed up as hell but you love her, and beg her to sort you out. Because, if you don't, she's going to be on the first train back to London.'

'Guy, I love you dearly, but don't interfere in things you don't understand.'

'I might be younger than you,' Guy shot back, 'but I've got a hell of a lot more sense.'

Xavier said nothing, simply plugged his computer back into the wall and switched it on. And he ignored the fact that Guy slammed the door so hard it nearly fell off its hinges.

Allegra didn't come in to work the next day. Which proved what Xavier had thought all along. He spent the next week telling himself that it was her loss, not his; though the fact that neither his secretary nor his brother were speaking to him annoyed him further. It unsettled him, too. Had he pushed her away? Or was he right, and she would never have settled here anyway?

The phone shrilled, and he answered it absently.

'Monsieur Lefèvre?'

'Yes?'

'It's Bernard Moreau from Vins Exceptionnels. Clos Quatre is your wine, yes?'

Xavier started paying attention. How had Vins Exceptionnels heard of his own private bottling? Unless it was something to do with Allegra's Rookie Vigneronne blog. 'Yes.'

'I'm delighted to tell you that it's been awarded a gold medal in this year's competition.'

'I beg your pardon?' How could it possibly have won a gold medal? He hadn't entered it.

'It's still a little young, but the judges think that in a year or two it will be absolutely superb.'

'I...uh... Thank you. I wasn't expecting this.' Because he hadn't known about the entry. But he had a pretty good idea who'd done it.

'We'll be in touch shortly with the official certification,' Bernard said. 'But we just wanted you to know. Well done.'

'*Merci beaucoup.*'

Xavier's head was spinning as he put the phone down. Allegra had entered his wine in the competition—his, not the AOC or the *vin de pays*. His baby. She'd done it without telling him, too, because she believed in him and she wanted the world to know it.

She believed in him.

The world seemed to tilt. He'd been so wrong, it was untrue. Yes, she'd left Les Trois Closes—but not for the reason that Chantal had left his father, or for the reason that Véra had left Guy. Allegra had left because he'd done what she'd thought he'd done ten years ago: he'd pushed her away. And, now he thought about it, he realised that she'd put so much into the vineyard—the new labels, the website and the blog, the tours of the vineyard that she'd publicised with the local tourist board. All that stuff she'd said in Paris about not being sure where she wanted to be had been an elaborate bluff, because she hadn't wanted to put pressure on him. At the time, he'd been too obtuse to take the hint and say to her that he wanted her to stay.

'Xavier? Are you all right?' Thérèse asked, pausing in his doorway.

'No. I'm an idiot.' He dragged a hand through his hair. 'Can you book me a flight to London, please?'

'London?'

'London,' he confirmed. 'And I don't care how much it costs.' He took his credit card from his wallet and handed it to her. 'I want the fastest flight to get me to Allegra. If anyone wants me, tell them to call me next week. I'm going to fetch my passport.'

When he returned, ten minutes later, Thérèse said, 'The quickest flight is from Paris. But you're better off

going by train—it'll save you time the other end, too.
Your ticket's ready to collect at Avignon.' She handed
the credit card back to him.

'You,' he told her, kissing her cheek, 'are wonderful.
Thank you.'

En route from Avignon, he called Hortense. It took
him a long time to persuade her, but eventually she gave
him Allegra's address in London. Then he flicked into
the Internet on his mobile phone and checked out the
route to Allegra's flat, memorising it.

The rest of the journey to Paris dragged—and the
minutes seemed to go by even more slowly on the way
to London. But at last he was at St Pancras station. At
this time of day, Xavier knew it'd be quicker to take the
Tube than a taxi to cross the city. He paused for just long
enough to buy an armful of flowers, then headed out to
Allegra's Docklands flat.

If she wasn't in, then he'd sit on the doorstep until
she came back.

And he hoped to hell that she'd give him the chance
to explain.

In Docklands, Xavier rang the bell on Allegra's door and
waited; but the woman who answered the door wasn't
Allegra.

'Sorry, I must have the wrong address,' he said. Hope-
fully this woman was a neighbour and would be able
to point him in the right direction. 'I was looking for
Allegra Beauchamp. I'm—'

'I know who you are,' she cut in, glaring at him.
'I'll see if Allie's available. Wait here.' She left the
door very slightly ajar, and he could hear her calling
Allegra's name.

On the one hand, he was glad that Allegra had a friend looking out for her. But he could really do without a gatekeeper. Having to relay messages through a hostile third party wasn't going to be ideal.

He could of course just walk straight in.

But he knew he didn't have the right. This was Allegra's territory, and he'd hurt her badly. So waiting was the right thing to do, even though he hated every second of it.

'You'd better come in,' the woman said when she returned to the door.

'Thank you.' He stepped inside and saw Allegra leaning against the wall, looking wary.

'I'll give you some space,' the woman said to Allegra. 'I'll be in the coffee bar across the road if you need me. I'll keep my mobile on.'

'Thanks, Gina.'

Allegra looked terrible. There were shadows beneath her eyes, her skin had none of the lustre it had held in France, and her soft curves had turned to angles again.

And it was all his fault.

He waited until Gina had closed the front door before he handed Allegra the flowers. 'Peace offering,' he said.

'Thank you,' she said. 'They're lovely. I'll put them in water.'

He followed her into the kitchen, where she found a vase and filled it with water.

'Allie, I know I don't deserve it, but I'm asking you to give me the chance I didn't give you. Would you hear me out?'

She finished arranging the flowers and turned to look at him. 'What's the point, Xav? You've made your position quite clear.'

'There's something else you need to know about that position,' he said. 'It's completely in the wrong.'

Allegra stared at him, wondering if she'd really heard that correctly. Xavier, admitting that he was wrong?

Maybe she was in some weird parallel universe.

'What are you doing here, Xav?' she asked. 'I mean, really?'

'I've come to apologise. For lots of things.' He blew out a breath. 'For pushing you away, for not trusting you, for not believing in you the way you believed in me.'

Everything she'd wanted to hear from him—before she'd given up and come back to England. 'What changed your mind?'

'A call from Vins Exceptionnels, to say we got a gold medal.'

The penny dropped. 'For Clos Quatre? Your wine got a gold?'

'*Our* wine,' he corrected. 'Yes.'

'That's fantastic!'

He reached out and took her hand. 'You believed in me enough to put my wine in the competition.'

'Without telling you,' she admitted with a twinge of guilt.

'You believed in me, Allie. You thought I was good enough. And it's made me realise something—I believe in you, too. I believe in us.' He took a deep breath. 'I know you like your independence and I know you want roots. I understand that—the way your parents dragged you about means that security's important to you. And

I also know you made your own roots in London. So if you want to live here, that's fine—we'll put a manager into the vineyard, and I'll move here.'

She was hardly able to believe what she was hearing. 'You'll move to London? For me?'

'For you,' he confirmed softly. 'Because France isn't home without you. I love the Ardèche, but without you it just isn't enough. I've been as miserable as hell without you. I know it's taken me too long to realise it, but my home's wherever you are. If that means living in London and getting a job working for someone else, then so be it.'

'You'd give up the vineyard for me?'

He nodded. 'Without you, Les Trois Closes is just an empty shell. I love you, Allie. I know I've hurt you, and I'm sorry. But if you'll give me the chance, I'll make it up to you.'

'You love me,' she said in wonder.

'I've loved you for years,' he said. 'I never really stopped. I realised that in Paris, and it scared the hell out of me. It still does, if I'm honest. Love makes you vulnerable.'

And he was admitting that vulnerability to her. Leaving his heart wide open and giving her the power to hurt him.

To trust her that much, and to put her needs above his beloved vineyard, he really must love her.

'I don't want you to get a job in London,' she said.

He untangled his fingers from hers, his expression grim. 'Too late? Well, I guess I deserve it—it's my own fault.'

She shook her head. 'That's not what I'm saying. You'd hate it here, Xav. You love Les Trois Closes.'

'I love you more, Allie. As long as you're with me, I don't care where I live or what I do.' He paused. 'Maybe we can find a place together. Somewhere of our own, where we can make good memories.'

'Where?'

'Wherever you're going to be happy.'

Although she'd been miserable since Paris, she'd been happy in the Ardèche before. Settled. And she knew how much Xavier loved his home. 'France,' she said. 'I want to live at Les Trois Closes and to make my home there with you.'

He took her hand again and drew it to his lips. 'I could build us a new house. By the lake, maybe. We could make a fresh start. You, me—and, if we're lucky enough, our children.'

He wanted children? With her?

'Allie?' With the pad of his thumb, he wiped away the single tear trickling down her cheek. 'Don't cry.'

'Xav, I...' A second tear spilled over, and a third.

He wrapped his arms round her, cradling her against him. 'Don't cry, *ma belle*. I love you. Whatever it takes to make you happy, I'll do it.'

She swallowed hard. 'I'm not crying because I'm sad. I love you so much, Xav. And I didn't think you'd ever be able to love me back. I thought you were too broken.'

'I was. But you've healed me,' he said softly. He brushed his mouth against hers. 'Come home, Allie. Marry me and make a family with me. And I'll get you that dog you wanted so much.'

Home. A family. With Xavier. Everything she'd ever wanted. She reached up to kiss him back. 'Yes.'

CHAPTER TWELVE

GINA was sceptical when Allegra rang her to break the news, but after she'd returned to the flat and spent an hour or so grilling Xavier, she seemed mollified. 'So you're going to treat Allie as she deserves to be treated,' she said to Xavier, narrowing her eyes at him.

'Yes.' His fingers tightened round Allegra's. 'And, as she's agreed to marry me, I'm planning to buy her an engagement ring tomorrow. In Paris.'

'What's wrong with London?' Gina asked.

'Nothing. But Paris is…' He paused. 'Paris is special. And I have something in mind. But first I need to sort out a hotel for tonight.'

'You're not going to stay here with me?' Allegra asked, surprised and more than a little hurt.

'I didn't come here to impose on you, *ma belle*. I came to ask you to share your life with me. And there are some practical details I need to sort out.'

'What kind of practical details?'

'All I have with me is my passport, so for a start I need to buy a change of clothes.'

'You're telling me you came here on the spur of the moment?' She found that hard to believe; no way would Xavier be that spontaneous.

'I wanted the rest of my life to start right now,' he said, surprising her further. 'So, yes.'

'I have a washer-dryer,' Allegra said.

As if he remembered exactly what had happened when he'd put their wet clothes in his washing machine, Xavier coloured spectactularly.

'I'm not going to ask,' Gina said, laughing.

'Thank you. I think,' Xavier said. 'So, if I can borrow your washing machine later, Allie, can I take you both out to dinner this evening?'

'Normally,' Gina said, 'I'd be polite and say no to playing gooseberry. But as you're going to whisk my best friend back to France tomorrow and I have no idea when I'll get the chance to see her again—yes, please.'

Xavier smiled. 'You have an open invitation to come and stay whenever you like.'

After dinner, Xavier insisted on putting Gina in a taxi back to her own flat. He walked hand in hand with Allegra back to hers. She enjoyed peeling his clothes off and putting them in her washing machine; and he responded by making love to her slowly and tenderly, until she felt as if her bones had melted.

'I love you,' he said softly. 'I love you more than I knew it was possible to love anyone.'

'I love you, too.' She stroked his face. 'And I knew you'd get the gold medal. I told you how good your wine was. Your dad would've been so proud of you.'

'And Harry would've been proud of you. Look at the way you've made people take notice of our vineyard.' He paused. 'Do we have to wait until our new house is built before we get married?'

'No. We can live at Harry's.' She nestled closer to him. 'But if we want my parents to turn up to the wedding, we'll have to fit it around their schedule, so that might be a while in the future.'

'That's up to you, *ma belle*.' He stole a kiss. 'If I had my way, I'd marry you tomorrow. But I thought maybe we could have a ceremony in the village church.'

'So Harry and your dad will sort of be there. I'd like that,' she said.

The next morning, Xavier brought Allegra coffee and toast in bed, then proceeded to book their flights and a hotel room.

'We're staying in Paris tonight?' she asked.

'Yes. I know it's not Christmas, but I always planned to propose to you in Paris. This is…just a little late.'

She smiled. 'Hey. No regrets. We've learned from the past.'

He kissed her. 'I love you. And I'm buying you a dress to wear, so you don't have to pack a thing. Not even your toothbrush,' he said. 'The hotel will deal with everything.'

'That sounds a bit extravagant,' she said. She revised her opinion to 'extremely' when the taxi stopped outside their hotel in Paris and Xavier collected the key to their suite. She'd expected maybe a nice room with a four-poster; she hadn't expected a circular Italian marble bath with a view of Montmartre, a huge bed with a gold silk canopy, a living room with one glass wall and an incredible view over the Seine, and a rooftop terrace with a view over Paris.

'Xav, this is just *stunning*,' she breathed.

'Like you.' He stole a kiss. 'Come on. We have shopping to do.' Which involved the Champs-Elysées, pure silk underwear, and the most beautiful dress and shoes Allegra had ever seen, both in midnight-blue silk.

Finally, he took her into an exclusive jeweller's on the Place Vendôme, where she noticed that the jewellery had no price tags.

'Xav, this is too m—' she began.

He pressed his forefinger lightly to her lips, stopping the words. 'Stop worrying. It's fine. I want you to choose something you like.'

She tried on several different rings, but the one she liked best was a simple twist of platinum with a brilliant-cut diamond in the centre. And it was the perfect fit, not even needing any alteration.

'This was meant to be,' Xavier said simply, and bought it.

They spent the rest of the afternoon playing tourist in the sunshine, sipped aperitifs overlooking the Seine, and then Xavier suggested that they went back to the hotel to change.

Allegra already guessed that he was going to give her the ring tonight. Though where he'd choose to do it was another matter. The top of the Eiffel Tower, as he'd told her he once planned to do? Montmartre, his favourite part of the city? Under the Arc de Triomphe?

'First,' he said, 'I want to share something with you.' He ran a bath, adding a viscous golden liquid that made the water smell of honey and gave the water a deep topping of creamy bubbles. Then he slowly peeled off her clothes, kissing every centimetre of skin as he revealed it. She enjoyed returning the favour, and then he lifted her up and stepped into the bath with her.

The view was incredible: the white basilica of the Sacré-Coeur was in sharp relief against the deep blue of the sky.

'Xav, this is...' She shook her head, unable to find the words.

'This is you and me,' he said softly. 'And I wanted to spoil you a bit.'

He dipped his head to brush his mouth against hers, and his hand slid down her back, smoothing the curve of her spine. She wrapped her arms round him and deepened the kiss; the next thing she knew, he'd shifted and pulled her onto his lap so she was sitting astride him.

'Now that's decadent,' she teased.

'Mmm, and we have to stop.' He kissed the hollows of her collarbones. 'I need to get a condom.'

'No, you don't. I don't want any more barriers between us. I want all of you, Xav.'

'*Dieu*, how I love you, Allegra Beauchamp,' he said, and kissed her hard.

She lifted herself slightly, slid her hand round his shaft, and then eased down on him.

'Oh, yes.' His breath was a hiss of pure pleasure. 'Do you have any idea how incredible you feel?'

'About as incredible as you do.' And, seeing the passion in his gaze, she believed now that he loved her as much as she loved him.

She began to move, and he cupped her buttocks, supporting her as she lifted up and lowered herself down. Her arms were round his neck, his mouth was plundering hers, and the tension inside her was coiling tighter and tighter and tighter until at last she hit the peak. She felt his body surge against hers, and knew he was there with her.

'You're amazing. And I love you more than words can say,' he said.

'Me, too.'

He coughed. 'You could try.'

She rubbed the tip of her nose against his. 'The first time I saw you, when I was eight years old, I decided that you were the man I was going to marry. I've loved you for years and years and years. Even when I told myself I didn't. And I'll love you for the rest of my life and beyond.'

'Glad to hear it,' he said, holding her close. 'We'd better get out of here, or we'll be like prunes.'

'I need to wash my hair.'

He kissed her lightly. 'Then I'll leave you, *ma belle*. Your things are all in your dressing room. Come and get me when you're ready.'

'Count on it,' she said as he climbed out of the bath and wrapped himself in a thick, fluffy bath sheet.

'You look fantastic,' he said when she finally emerged from her dressing room.

'So do you.' In a well-cut dark suit, white shirt and a sober silk tie, he looked every millimetre the Parisian socialite, sophisticated and urbane. And yet she knew the other side of him, the scruffy vigneron who was equally at home making love with her in a meadow of wild flowers. Both sides of him made her heart beat faster.

'May I have the pleasure of your company for dinner this evening, Mademoiselle Beauchamp?' he asked.

'*Bien sûr*, Monsieur Lefèvre,' she said with a smile.

He tucked her arm through his. But just when she thought he was going to open the door to their private lift and take her out to Paris, instead he led her onto the terrace. A table had been set for them with a white damask tablecloth, a silver candelabrum with vanilla-scented candles, and a silver bowl full of the palest pink roses. The shrubs by their table were festooned with tiny white fairy lights.

From the terrace, they could see most of the city, and in the dusk the buildings were beginning to light up.

'Welcome to the City of Light,' he said softly. 'I want it to be an evening you'll remember,' he told her, his eyes glittering. 'Tonight's special.'

The night they were finally committing to each other. A shiver of mingled delight and apprehension rippled down her spine.

The meal was fabulous—a rosette of avocado with grapefruit and shrimps, Sole Meunière with a selection of perfectly cooked vegetables, and the best crème brûlée she'd ever tasted. Particularly as Xavier insisted on sharing a spoon with her, while she was sitting on his lap.

And then finally, after rich, dark coffee, Xavier took a midnight-blue velvet box from his pocket and dropped to one knee beside her. Opening the box and offering her the ring, he asked, 'Allegra—will you be my wife, the love of my life and my equal partner, for the rest of our days?'

'Yes,' she said.

And sealed it with a kiss.

Coming Next Month

from **Harlequin Presents®**. Available December 28, 2010.

Coming Next Month

from **Harlequin Presents® EXTRA**. Available January 11, 2011.

HPECNM1210

REQUEST YOUR FREE BOOKS!

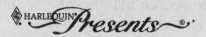

2 FREE NOVELS PLUS
2 FREE GIFTS!

YES! Please send me 2 FREE Harlequin Presents® novels and my 2 FREE gifts (gifts are worth about $10). After receiving them, if I don't wish to receive any more books, I can return the shipping statement marked "cancel." If I don't cancel, I will receive 6 brand-new novels every month and be billed just $4.05 per book in the U.S. or $4.74 per book in Canada. That's a saving of at least 15% off the cover price! It's quite a bargain! Shipping and handling is just 50¢ per book.* I understand that accepting the 2 free books and gifts places me under no obligation to buy anything. I can always return a shipment and cancel at any time. Even if I never buy another book, the two free books and gifts are mine to keep forever.

106/306 HDN E5M4

Name _____ (PLEASE PRINT) _____

Address _____ Apt. # _____

City _____ State/Prov. _____ Zip/Postal Code _____

Signature (if under 18, a parent or guardian must sign)

Mail to the **Harlequin Reader Service:**
IN U.S.A.: P.O. Box 1867, Buffalo, NY 14240-1867
IN CANADA: P.O. Box 609, Fort Erie, Ontario L2A 5X3

Not valid for current subscribers to Harlequin Presents books.

Are you a current subscriber to Harlequin Presents books and want to receive the larger-print edition? Call 1-800-873-8635 today!

* Terms and prices subject to change without notice. Prices do not include applicable taxes. N.Y. residents add applicable sales tax. Canadian residents will be charged applicable provincial taxes and GST. Offer not valid in Quebec. This offer is limited to one order per household. All orders subject to approval. Credit or debit balances in a customer's account(s) may be offset by any other outstanding balance owed by or to the customer. Please allow 4 to 6 weeks for delivery. Offer available while quantities last.

Your Privacy: Harlequin Books is committed to protecting your privacy. Our Privacy Policy is available online at www.eHarlequin.com or upon request from the Reader Service. From time to time we make our lists of customers available to reputable third parties who may have a product or service of interest to you. If you would prefer we not share your name and address, please check here. ☐

Help us get it right—We strive for accurate, respectful and relevant communications. To clarify or modify your communication preferences, visit us at www.ReaderService.com/consumerschoice.

HP10R

HARLEQUIN®

A *Romance*

FOR EVERY MOOD™

Spotlight on
Classic

Quintessential, modern love stories
that are romance at its finest.

See the next page
to enjoy a sneak peek from
the Harlequin Presents® series.

"LET ME GET THIS STRAIGHT. Are you actually suggesting that I would stoop to that kind of game playing?"

Saul came out from behind his desk and walked toward her. Giselle could smell his hot male scent and it was making her dizzy, igniting a low, dull, pulsing ache that was taking over her whole body.

Giselle defended her suspicions. "You don't want me here."

"No," Saul agreed, "I don't."

And then he did what he had sworn he would not do, cursing himself beneath his breath as he reached for her, pulling her fiercely into his arms and kissing her with all the pent-up fury she had aroused in him from the moment he had first seen her.

Giselle certainly *wanted* to resist him. But the hand she raised to push him away developed a will of its own and was sliding along his bare arm beneath the sleeve of his shirt, and the body that should have been arching away from him was instead melting into him.

Beneath the pressure of his kiss he could feel and taste her gasp of undeniable response to him. He wanted to devour her, take her and drive them both until they were equally satiated—even whilst the anger within him that she should make him feel that way roared and burned its resentment of his need.

She was helpless, Giselle recognized, totally unable to withstand the storm lashing at her, able only to cling to the man who was the cause of it and pray that she would survive.

Somewhere else in the building a door banged. The sound exploded into the sensual tension that had enclosed them, driving them apart. Saul's chest was rising and falling as he fought for control; Giselle's whole body was trembling.

Without a word she turned and ran.

Find out what happens when Saul and Giselle succumb to their irresistible desire in

THE RELUCTANT SURRENDER

Available January 2011 from Harlequin Presents®

HPEXP0111

Love Inspired

Bestselling author

JILLIAN HART

brings readers another heartwarming story
from

the
GRANGER
FAMILY
RANCH

To fulfill a sick boy's wish, rodeo star Tucker Granger surprises
little Owen in the hospital. And no one is more surprised than
single mother Sierra Baker. But somehow Tucker ropes her heart
and fills it with hope. Hope that this country girl and her son
can lasso the roaming bronc rider into their family forever.

Look for
His Country Girl

Available January
wherever books are sold.

www.SteepleHill.com

Steeple
Hill®

LI87643